1

Oregon, 1879

J.J. 'Jack' Marric alighted in front of the saloon just as dusk settled in over Roseburg. After nine days of riding, he was thoroughly exhausted; he wanted nothing more than a shot of rye and, after that, a good night's sleep.

The saloon was on the southern edge of town. As he tied his reins over the hitching post, Marric looked up the muddy street. He spotted a hotel a block away. That, he decided, would be his next destination. He patted his chestnut mare on the neck and then climbed the warped steps up to the plank sidewalk. The smell of tobacco smoke drifted over the batwing doors of the saloon. Marric shouldered his way into the establishment and paused, his eyes sweeping over the room.

There were ten or twelve men there.

Half of them were leaning on the bar, with the other half gathered around a large table, playing a subdued poker game. One or two of the patrons turned their gazes to the newcomer, then went back to their whiskey or cards. That suited Marric just fine. He wasn't in the mood for conversation anyway.

He crossed to the bar and removed his Stetson as he sat down on a stool. The barkeep finished wiping up a glass before making his way down to Marric. He was an elderly man with a thick shock of snow-white hair. His alert eyes belied his apparent physical frailty.

'Evening, mister,' he said. 'What can I get you?'

'Whiskey,' Marric replied. 'The best you got.'

The old man smiled. 'Coming right up.'

A few moments later, a shot glass appeared on the bar. The barkeep splashed liquor into it and Marric downed it immediately.

'Another?' the man asked.

THE BOOT HILL BREED

Jack Marric is returning to his family home after learning of his mother's illness. But a decision to stop for a drink at a saloon results in him getting into a fight with and killing two men who are bullying the elderly saloon-keeper. Jack is enthusiastically welcomed home by his family, but unbeknown to him, he has been followed by the brother of the two dead men, who is now hell-bent on revenge and will kill anyone who gets in his way. Soon the whole family are under threat because of Jack's act of courage . . .

NED OAKS

THE
BOOT HILL
BREED

Complete and Unabridged

LINFORD
Leicester

First published in Great Britain in 2016 by
Robert Hale
an imprint of The Crowood Press
Wiltshire

First Linford Edition
published 2018
by arrangement with
The Crowood Press
Wiltshire

A catalogue record for this book is available
from the British Library.

ISBN 978–1–4448–3886–2

Published by
F. A. Thorpe (Publishing)
Anstey, Leicestershire

Set by Words & Graphics Ltd.
Anstey, Leicestershire
Printed and bound in Great Britain by
T. J. International Ltd., Padstow, Cornwall

This book is printed on acid-free paper

Marric nodded. 'Please.'

When he had refilled the glass, the barkeep moved down the bar to help some other customers. Marric relaxed and sipped at his second drink. He glanced into the mirror behind the bar, thinking that he could use a hot bath and a shave.

He was a large man, just over six feet tall. Still in his early thirties, his skin was dark and lined from years of laboring outdoors, both in ranch work and in mining. His face was further darkened by several days' worth of stubble. He had a narrow nose that hooked slightly, ending in a point. His pale green eyes were probably his most notable and memorable feature. They told you everything you needed to know about how Jack Marric felt. When he was pleased, they sparkled with good humor. When he was angry, they glinted like chips of ice.

He was dressed in range clothes — Levi's, boots, a woolen shirt, and a sheepskin coat. In the holster on his right hip was a large Navy Colt, strapped to his thigh by a narrow strip of leather. Gunplay wasn't Marric's business, but he was highly skilled with a pistol, and had been since he was a boy. At times people had mistaken him for a cowpunch with no gun sense; on those occasions they had invariably learned how wrong they were.

Marric waved the barkeep over and, draining his shot glass, asked for another. The man complied.

'You from around here, feller?' he asked amiably.

Marric shook his head. 'I'm from Jasper,' he explained. 'A little east of Springfield.'

'Jasper,' the barkeep muttered, as if searching his mind. 'You know, I think I passed through there once, a long time ago.'

'It ain't much to see.'

'No, it was a real small place. What brings you to Roseburg?'

Marric didn't normally talk with people he didn't know, but he realized the old man was just making idle conversation to pass the time.

'Well, I spent the last six years in California, doing a little of this and a little of that,' he said. 'Got a telegram from my pa last week telling me my ma wasn't doing so good. I decided it was time to come home for a spell.'

'Sorry to hear about your ma. My wife died two years ago next month. It ain't been the same without her, I'll tell you that.'

Marric nodded slowly. 'I've been away too long. It'll be good to see the family again.'

'Family's important. Hell, it's probably the most important thing.' The barkeep raised his eyes as the batwings parted and two men entered the saloon. 'Aw, damn it. The Harper boys are here. I better go tend to them. I'll give you some more whiskey here in a minute.'

The unease in the man's voice caused Marric to look in the mirror. In the reflection he could see two dirty men standing side-by-side just inside the room. They looked like twins. There was an unmistakable aura of danger and malevolence about them, evident even from where Marric was sitting. They both seemed to sneer as they glanced around the saloon. He lowered his gaze back to his drink and sipped it, wondering who these Harpers were and why they made the barkeep so nervous.

They strode up to the bar a couple yards to Marric's right. The one nearest him slapped his hand down hard on the counter.

'Beer, Glidden!' he cried.

His brother laughed. 'Make that two beers, old man. And get stepping!'

They were obviously already drunk; Marric could smell whiskey fumes emanating from them. He already didn't like them. They acted like they owned the saloon, and like the man behind the bar was their servant. He assumed they were big fish in the little pond that was Roseburg.

Glidden filled two glasses with beer

and placed them on the counter before the Harper brothers. Neither thanked him as they lifted the drinks and gulped the liquid down. They slammed the empty glasses on to the bar simultaneously.

Marric wondered if this was some kind of performance they were putting on for the other patrons of the saloon. He noted a new sort of tension in the atmosphere. The men at the poker table were quieter than they had been, each studying his cards as if keenly aware of the presence of the Harpers. At the bar, one of the men nearest to the brothers moved down a few feet further away from where they stood.

The Harper closest to Marric belched loudly as he sleeved foam away from his grimy lips.

'Another round for me and my brother,' he demanded.

Glidden hesitated for a moment, then complied. The brothers drained the beer and again slammed the glasses on to the counter. They seemed to be playing a game with the old barkeep.

'I know you're not going to make us ask for a third, Glidden.'

This time it was the other brother speaking. Marric watched him in the mirror.

'Boys, you know I got no problem serving you,' Glidden said, his voice steady despite his fear. 'It's just that you ain't paid your tab in three months. I've dispensed a lot of beer and liquor your way, but I ain't seen a penny. I'm . . .' Here he hesitated again, and Marric noticed the flinty expressions on both of the Harpers' faces. 'I'm going to have to cut you both off until you pay.'

The silence in the room was deafening. The head of every other man in the saloon turned to observe the exchange at the bar. Only Marric seemed indifferent, although his narrowed eyes were watching the Harper brothers in the mirror behind the bar.

'Did you hear that, Matt?' the brother nearest to Marric asked incredulously.

8

'I sure did, Gil,' said Matt. 'I believe old Glidden just told us we're no longer welcome here.'

'Now, boys,' Glidden said. 'I didn't say y'all ain't welcome. All I said was that before I can serve you again, you're going to have to pay off your tab.' He swallowed. 'That's all.'

'You don't think we're good for the money?' Matt asked. Marric thought he was the leader of the two siblings. 'Them's hurtful words.'

'Very hurtful,' Gil said with a smirk. 'After all the years you've known us, Glidden.'

'You got to understand,' Glidden pleaded. 'A man's got to make a living, and I can't do that if I give away beer and whiskey for free.'

'Damn it, we'll give you your damn money,' Matt said. 'You don't have to insult us.'

'Like I said — ' Glidden began, but before he could finish his words were cut off, along with his air supply, by the massive right hand of Gil Harper, who leaned across the counter and gripped the elderly man by his neck. His fingers closed savagely around Glidden's throat, and he pulled the man toward him, yanking him halfway across the counter.

'We're done listening to your damn mouth, old timer,' said Gil through clenched teeth. His face was flushed with alcohol and rage. 'You're going to fill those damn glasses and, by God, you'll keep filling them until we tell you to stop. Savvy?'

He released the barkeep, shoving him hard away from the bar. Glidden crashed against the shelves behind him, knocking a few bottles on to the plank floor. The glass shattered around his feet as he struggled for breath, his hands feeling gingerly at his neck.

'More beer, goddamn it!' Matt Harper bellowed.

'Damn, Glidden — looks like we got ourselves a couple of half-wits here, don't we?'

Jack Marric's voice filled the room.

10

He remained on his stool, looking relaxed. He had turned his head slightly and fixed his gaze on the Harper brothers. They, along with every other man in the room, were now staring at him.

With dangerous, slitted eyes, Matt Harper said, 'Did I just hear you right, stranger?'

Marric turned his shot glass a couple times, holding it delicately between his fingers. Then he lifted it to his lips and tossed back the remaining whiskey before his eyes locked on those of Matt Harper.

'Beats me. You hard of hearing as well as stupid?' he asked.

'Judas priest!' sputtered Gil. 'Did you hear that, Matt?'

'You must be part deaf, too,' Marric retorted. 'Or maybe neither of you understands plain English.' He stepped off his stool and leaned against the bar, resting his weight on his left elbow. 'The old man said you're cut off. I'm pretty he sure he owns this place, not you two. So unless you're going to give the man his money, I suggest you both head on out and find refreshment elsewhere.' Marric flicked his eyes to the men at the poker table. Their faces expressed disbelief.

No wonder these Harper boys strut around the way they do, he thought. *They got everyone scared of their own shadows.*

'You got a real smart mouth there, mister,' Matt said.

Marric thought he looked a little unsure of himself. The Harper brothers were definitely not used to being challenged. Marric's lips formed a half-grin. 'I guess I just don't like seeing some two-bit bully trying to be tough with an old man who's half his size.' He shrugged. 'But hell, maybe that's the way they do things here in Roseburg.'

Gil Harper wet his lips with his tongue, the alcohol dulling his already notably slow mental capacity. He wasn't sure what to make of the situation, but he had confidence that Matt would know the proper course of action.

'Glidden insulted us,' he said. 'We ain't going to take that from no one.'

'He didn't insult you,' Marric said. 'You insult him by stealing his liquor.'

'We ain't stealing a damn thing!' said Matt.

'If you ain't paying the man, then you're stealing from him. Does that make sense to you or do I have to draw you a picture?'

Matt Harper stepped away from the bar and moved toward Jack Marric.

'I've had about enough of your mouth,' he said, reaching out and grabbing the front of Marric's sheepskin.

He was a strong man, a few inches taller and at least twenty pounds heavier than Marric. His hand gripped the coat and he pulled back his other arm and made a fist. Before he could drive it into Marric's face, the latter responded with a combination of speed and power that stunned the onlookers in the saloon.

He drove his fist into Matt's throat, and as the man clawed at his neck, his eyes bulging with shock and pain, Marric followed up with a brutal series of punches to the abdomen. Matt folded at the waist, staying on his feet for only a few seconds before his knees buckled and he went down.

Marric moved away from the fallen man, looking up just in time to see Gil Harper reach down for the pistol in his holster.

'I would think twice about that if I were you,' Marric said. 'Unless you're keen to die right here, in front of everyone.'

A bead of sweat rolled down Gil's right cheek. Marric could almost hear the rusty gears turning in the man's mind, and then Gil's lip curled with contempt and he gripped the butt of his pistol and dragged the gun upwards.

In one swift, fluid motion, Marric's right hand streaked down to his Navy Colt. He palmed it and cleared leather just as Gil thumbed back the hammer of his gun, leveling it at Marric. Marric's left hand chopped at the hammer of his Colt, sending three rapid shots into Gil Harper's sternum. The mortally wounded man gasped, dropping his gun on to the floor. He took a couple of stumbling steps backward, knocking over a stool, and then he went down, hitting the floor with a loud thud.

Marric's fight with the Harper brothers had unfolded in a matter of seconds. Both men lay unmoving on the floor, one dead and the other apparently unconscious. The acrid scent of gun-smoke filled the room as Marric replaced his pistol in its holster and looked around the room. Every man was watching him with wide eyes, including the old man called Glidden.

Marric exhaled slowly. 'Anyone want to say that wasn't self-defense?' he asked, examining each man in turn.

No one said anything until Marric met the gaze of the poker dealer on the far side of the table.

'No question about it, mister,' the dealer said. 'They went after you. You'd be dead if you hadn't done what you did.'

'Glad to hear it,' Marric said.

Glidden stepped forward and stood on his toes to look down at the two prone men on the floor in front of the bar.

'I don't think you'll find too many folks who like Matt and Gil Harper,' he said. 'Except their brother. I don't know where he is, but unless you want more trouble, I'd clear out.'

Marric pursed his lips thoughtfully. 'Makes sense,' he said. 'I don't go looking for trouble, as a rule.'

'Thank you kindly for coming to my aid, feller,' Glidden said. He glanced at the other customers. 'No one's ever done that for me before.'

'Seemed like the right thing to do at the time,' Marric said.

'Would you like one more shot before you go?'

Marric smiled crookedly. 'As long as

you make it a double.'

'You got it, friend.'

The old man filled two shot glasses with the amber fluid, and Marric despatched them quickly.

'I'll be on my way,' he announced, stepping over Matt Harper and walking toward the batwings.

He pushed through them and paused on the sidewalk outside. He felt for the makings and constructed a cigarette, his blunt fingers perfectly steady. He poked the smoke into his lips and thumb-snapped a vesta, inhaling deeply as the tobacco took flame. He descended the steps to the muddy street and put a foot in a stirrup. He was just about to climb into leather when he heard some commotion from within the saloon.

The anguished cries of Matt Harper echoed out into the street. The man had regained consciousness.

'Christ Almighty, that son of a bitch killed my brother!'

Marric put his boot back down in the

mud and stepped away from his horse. If there was shooting to be done, he didn't want the animal to be injured. He heard heavy boots scraping across the plank floor in the saloon, moving toward the batwings. A shadow partially blocked the light from within the bar, and then the doors flew outward as Matt burst through them, now hatless and frenzied, his pistol in his right hand. He saw Marric and began to raise the gun.

'You murdering polecat!' he screamed. 'You killed Gil!'

Without a word, Marric drew his pistol and fired from the hip with the uncanny accuracy that he had carefully honed over more than half of his life. The bullet struck Matt Harper dead centre in the forehead, killing him instantly. His glassy eyes rolled back in his head and he collapsed forward on to the boards of the sidewalk, his pistol slipping from his fingers and clattering down the steps into the mud of the street.

2

The rain began to pour down on Jack Marric as he stood in the street, staring at the body on the side-walk. Some of the men inside the saloon appeared in the doorway. Marric climbed the steps and stood under the awning, a few steps from Matt Harper's crumpled remains.

The crowd near the batwings parted and Glidden came out on to the sidewalk.

'This was self-defense, too,' he said. 'There ain't no one who can deny that.'

Marric's face was grim. 'I wish he'd stayed out cold a few more minutes.'

A man stepped out of the shadows of the alley beside the saloon, a pistol in his hand.

'That would have saved you a lot of trouble,' he said, stepping beneath the lantern that dangled on the wall by the saloon doors. The star on his chest reflected the light.

'Evening, Marshal Taylor,' said Glidden, turning toward the lawman.

The marshal grunted inscrutably, looking down at Matt Harper's corpse.

'Matt Harper,' he observed. 'I was making my final rounds for the night when I heard the ruckus. Should have known it'd be him or his brothers if there was shooting in town.' He shifted his eyes to Jack Marric, toward whom his pistol was pointed. 'I'm going to need you to draw that Colt and drop it.'

'It was self-defense,' Marric said.

'Maybe so,' Taylor said coolly. 'That'll be for me to judge.'

Marric slowly pulled out his gun and dropped it by his feet. A pool of blood was forming around Harper's head, and some of it dripped down between the gaps in the boards.

'His brother's inside,' Marric noted.

'He dead, too?' the marshal asked.

'I'm afraid so.'

Taylor scratched at his chin with a

forefinger. 'Hmmm — what about their other brother?'

'Haven't met him yet,' Marric said.

'They both pulled guns on this feller before he even cleared leather,' Glidden asserted. He jerked a thumb toward the men gathered behind him. 'They were all there. They saw it happen.'

'That so?' inquired Taylor. The group muttered assent. 'Fair enough. I'm going to take a look at Gil.' He holstered his weapon and walked into the saloon, leaving Marric on the sidewalk. When he emerged, he addressed the solemn-looking saloon patrons. 'I want every man who was in Glidden's place tonight to be at my office in the morning so I can take your statements.' He looked at the barkeep. 'That includes you, Glidden.'

'I'll be there,' the old man said.

Marshal Taylor leaned forward and picked up Marric's gun.

'You come along with me to the law office,' he said. 'I'm going to take your statement tonight. If none of these fellers says you killed in cold blood, then I'll let you go.'

Marric was clearly not pleased, but he recognized the futility of arguing.

'Lead the way, Marshal. I'll help however I can.'

'Good.' Taylor gestured up the sidewalk in the direction of the hotel where Marric had planned to spend the night. 'Glidden, will you take his horse to the livery?'

'Yes, sir,' said Glidden.

Marric pivoted and began walking up the side-walk with the lawman trailing close behind. As they passed the hotel, they saw a woman standing near the window of the lobby, concern etched upon her face. Taylor smiled at her and dipped his hat reassuringly.

The marshal's office, which was just past the hotel, consisted of a small room with a desk and two chairs. There was a large, heavy door in the centre of the back wall; it led to the cell block, which contained two very small cells. After they had entered the office, Taylor shut the door and sat down behind the desk. He pointed to the chair across from him.

'Have a seat,' he said, pulling open a drawer and removing a pencil and a sheet of paper.

Marric sat down and folded his hands in front of him. He studied Taylor and concluded that he was probably an honest lawman, and definitely serious about his work. Taylor was a small man whose clean-shaven cheeks glowed pinkly in the light of the lantern on his desk. He exuded efficiency. Marric figured the marshal was probably somewhere in his fifties, despite his youthful appearance.

'Your name?' asked Taylor.

'John James Marric.'

'Your age?'

'Thirty-two.'

'Where are you from?'

'Jasper, Oregon.'

Taylor's pencil made rapid scratching noises on the paper as he wrote.

'What brings you to Roseburg?'

'I was coming home from California.'

'What for?'

'My ma took sick. I'm coming home to see her.'

'What happened tonight at the saloon?'

'I stopped in for a few shots of whiskey. I was planning on heading over to the hotel afterwards. Everything was fine until the Harper boys showed up, a few minutes after I got there. They were drunk and they started harassing that feller named Glidden. I let it go for a bit, but when one of them reached out grabbed him by the neck, I exchanged some words with them.'

Taylor arched an eyebrow. 'I suppose they didn't take kindly to that.'

'No, they didn't. All I wanted them to do was leave the old feller alone. They decided to push it a little further. The one named Matt put his hands on me and I knocked him out. Gil pulled a gun and I shot him. Matt was still out cold when I went outside to leave. I was just about in the saddle when he came out with his gun. It was him or me.'

About twenty seconds elapsed before Taylor finished scrawling. When he was done, he paused and looked over what he had written, then looked up at Marric.

'You read?' he asked.

'Yes, I can read.'

'The Harper brothers couldn't.' He handed the sheet of paper over to Marric. 'If this looks truthful to you, then I'll have you sign it. You'll have to spend one night in a cell here, and then when the men come tomorrow I'll take their statements. Unless there's some conflict, I'll release you and you can be on your way.'

Marric rubbed a hand across his bristly jaw. 'All right,' he said. He read the statement and then signed it.

Taylor took the paper and pencil and put them back in the drawer. He rose and showed Marric into the cell block. Marric walked into the first open cell and seated himself on the cot. There was a blanket folded at the end of it.

'I appreciate your cooperation,' Taylor said. 'The Harpers have been raising hell here ever since they were little kids.'

Marric said, 'I heard they had another brother.'

'Yes, they do,' said Taylor in a mildly pensive tone. 'I'd almost forgot about him. Wonder where he was tonight. He usually runs around with them. Name's Chet.'

'He as bad as Matt and Gil?'

'Worse.' Taylor closed the cell door and locked it. 'All right, then — I'll be seeing you in the morning. I got to go back and have the undertaker collect those bodies.'

The marshal turned and passed through into the front office. He closed the cell block door and Marric heard the key turn in it.

The prisoner removed his boots and gunbelt and placed them on the floor, along with his hat. He lay back on the cot, staring at the ceiling. He was sound asleep within five minutes.

★ ★ ★

By nine o'clock the next morning Marshal John Taylor had completed taking statements from the witnesses at the saloon. He came into the cell block and opened the barred door to Jack Marric's cell.

'All finished,' he said. 'There's no question that the brothers started the entire thing. You're free to go.'

Marric rose, stretching his limbs. It hadn't been a comfortable night. He slipped on his boots and his gunbelt and walked with the marshal into the front office.

'Your horse is out front,' Taylor said.

Marric pushed his hat firmly down on his head. 'Thanks for the fair treatment, Marshal. I've known some lawmen who weren't as conscientious about getting to the truth as you are.'

Taylor spread his hands. 'If a man can't be impartial he should find a different line of work.'

Marric smiled and nodded, and then

walked out to the sidewalk. It was a brisk fall morning, and the sun shining brightly above the small town hadn't dispelled the chill in the air. He saw his horse tied to the hitching post and descended the steps into the street.

There was considerable activity in the shops and offices around him. Most people seemed indifferent to his presence, but a few stopped and regarded him curiously before moving on. Marric understood how quickly word travelled in small towns like Roseburg.

As he climbed into the saddle, Marric saw a fat, very well-dressed man approaching him. The man stopped near the hitching post and removed his small brown hat. He had neatly trimmed salt-and-pepper hair and a ruddy face. Judging from the suit he wore, Marric took him for a lawyer or a prominent businessman of some sort.

'Excuse me, sir,' the man said. 'I understand you're the man who killed the Harper brothers last night?'

Marric's face hardened. 'It was

self-defense,' he said. 'The marshal has talked to the witnesses and cleared me.'

The man raised a hand. 'Of course, sir. I didn't mean to say that you provoked it.'

'Fine,' said Marric, frowning slightly. 'What can I do for you? I have places to be.'

'My name is Martin Lange — perhaps you've heard of me?'

'Afraid not.'

For a brief moment, Lange looked irritated. 'All right, then. I am the editor and publisher of the newspaper here in Roseburg — the Gazette. Perhaps you've heard of that?'

'Afraid not.'

'It has the biggest circulation of any journalistic publication in this part of Oregon.'

'I don't doubt it. What's that got to do with me?'

'Well, I was wondering if you would agree to be interviewed for tomorrow's edition. The Harper brothers were very

well known in these parts. Troublemak-
ers, the whole lot of them. I figured
maybe you'd like to give your side of
the story — let the people know what
happened, direct from the man himself.'

Marric's frown was much more
pronounced now. 'Afraid not,' he said.

He neck-reined his horse and headed
up the street, feeling Lange's currant-
like eyes boring into his back. A wave of
disgust came over him. He had no
particular feelings for the Harper
brothers; they were clearly violent thugs
who enjoyed pushing people around.
But he hadn't wanted to kill them, and
he derived no pleasure from having
done so. He was sure that Lange's
motivation was to sensationalize the
men's deaths and sell more copies of
his newspaper in the process.

As he passed the last few houses on
the outskirts of town, Marric felt quite
relieved to leave Roseburg behind.

★　★　★

The rest of the day passed quietly for Marshal Taylor.

He, too, was approached by Martin Lange, who was eager to hear the marshal's account of the shootings. Taylor declined. He met with Roseburg's only judge and told him about the events of the previous evening. The judge concurred with Taylor's decision not to pursue charges against Jack Marric.

After eating lunch at home with his wife, Taylor made his afternoon rounds. He passed some time looking over the new Wanted dodgers that had been delivered from Salem before locking up the office and making his evening rounds. As was generally the case, Roseburg was quiet.

Taylor was pleased not to be dealing with any more bloodshed, although he, like virtually all the town's residents, had lost no sleep over the Harper brothers. At best, they were unpredictable and prone to violence. At worst, they might have been responsible for a couple of unsolved murders in the Roseburg area dating back more than five years. Taylor had his suspicions, but the lack of witnesses and evidence in each case had precluded arresting and charging the brothers. He was amused by the thought that a stranger had eliminated two of the three most dangerous men in town, only minutes after arriving. Jack Marric had done Roseburg an inadvertent favor, and most of the people in town were grateful.

Dusk had given way to darkness by the time Taylor opened the gate to his front yard and began to walk toward the house. He could see a light around back, coming from the kitchen window. He was hungry and looking forward to a peaceful evening with his wife.

He moved to the left and passed the rose bushes before reaching the narrow strip of lawn on the side of the house. The area was immersed in darkness, and Taylor was about halfway to the back when the large laurel bush that bordered the fence seemed to part. He saw movement in his peripheral vision and turned, his hand moving instinctively toward his pistol. But he was too late.

A massive arm encircled his neck and pulled him backward. His hands reached up and he tried to pry the arm from his throat, but the man behind him was too powerful. He reached down to grab his pistol and a vice-like hand gripped his wrist.

Taylor felt hot, rancid breath near his ear as his attacker spoke.

'Evening, Marshal,' the voice said.

The lawman recognized it instantly, and his blood ran cold. It was Chet Harper, the brother of the two dead men. Taylor struggled to speak, but the pressure on his neck didn't allow him to utter a sound. Darkness began to overtake him and he fought to maintain consciousness.

'Before I kill you, I just wanted you to know I heard about you letting the feller who killed my brothers go free. I don't appreciate that. I don't care if they started it or not — no one kills a Harper and walks. Now you're going to pay for what he did.'

Spittle flew from Taylor's lips as he tried to pull air into his lungs. A brief flash of reflected light was the last thing he saw before he died. It was a knife, thin and razor-sharp.

Chet Harper drove the knife into Taylor's throat, then removed his other arm from the man's neck. He grabbed the marshal's hair and pulled his head back, leaving his neck fully exposed. The slashing of his throat was deep and quick, executed with such power that it nicked Taylor's spine and nearly decapitated him. Harper released Taylor, who fell into the damp grass beside the laurel bush. After making a few grotesque gurgling sounds, the marshal of Roseburg became silent.

3

It wasn't until the afternoon of the day after his release from the Roseburg jail that Jack Marric drew reins at the edge of his family's property. The Marric place was located along the McKenzie River on the edge of Jasper, a miniscule hamlet a few miles east of Springfield.

The Marrics had owned their seventy acres here for more than three decades. Floyd Marric, Jack's father, had worked as a logger first, and then eventually moved up to become the manager of one of the largest lumber mills in this area of the Willamette Valley. He had married Sarah, Jack's mother, and bought the property just after he got his first promotion at the mill. They had raised Jack and his younger sister, Marijo, in the log cabin that Floyd had constructed here with his own hands.

Marric sat his horse at the edge of

the forest, just where the trees met the yard. In the six years since he had left Jasper, the house had grown; there was a large veranda across the front of the house, made of river rock. One room appeared to have been added at the back. Seeing his childhood home stirred powerful emotions in Jack Marric. It was a place of happiness and security, of domestic tranquility. He often thought of how lucky he had been to have been born and raised in that cabin.

He kneed his mount out of the trees and approached the veranda. He was still ten yards away when the door opened and a tiny woman with silver hair emerged from inside. She walked to the edge of the porch and shielded her eyes from the sun, looking in Marric's direction. He smiled and waved, and a joyous expression spread across the woman's face.

'Jack!' she cried.

He pulled leather near the bottom step and bounded from the saddle.

'I'm back, Ma,' he said.

Tears started to pool in his eyes, but he quickly blinked them away. Sarah Marric was gaunt, her skin like parchment.

Yes, he thought. *She really is sick.*

He fought off the feeling of despair that filled his chest as he put his arms around his mother. Acutely conscious of her fragility, he was careful not to squeeze her too hard.

She put her hands on his face and gazed at him. 'Look at you,' she said. 'I always think of you as a boy, but you've been a man for so long now.'

Marric laughed. 'Well, at least for a few weeks.' A cold wind blew across the veranda and Sarah shivered. 'Let's go in, Ma.'

She agreed, and he tied his reins to a post near the steps. As he crossed the threshold into the living room, he felt as if he were moving back in time. Everything seemed the same: the furnishings, the big rug on the floor — even the smell, a pleasant mixture of baked goods and his father's pipe tobacco.

'Do you want some coffee?' his mother asked.

'That sounds good.'

They passed through the living room into the kitchen and his mother began boiling coffee as Marric sat down at the table. A large brown cat with black stripes wandered into the kitchen from the hallway and began to rub its face on the side of his leg. Marric laughed and scratched the animal on the back of the neck.

'I'll be — Rufus is still alive and kicking, huh?' he asked.

Sarah laughed. 'Oh, he's still alive. Ornery as ever, too!'

'He must be, what — thirteen or fourteen years old now?'

'Something like that.'

Marric watched his mother as she poured coffee in two tin mugs and brought them over to the table. She handed one to him and sat down.

'How are you feeling, Ma?' he asked.

'Some days I feel fine,' she said. She took a sip from her mug. 'Other days I feel awful.'

'How do you feel today?'

Sarah patted his hand. 'Today is a good day.'

Marric looked down into his coffee, watching the steam rise.

'How long has this been going on?' he asked.

'About four months. I just started losing weight and no matter how much I ate, I couldn't keep it on.' She pulled her shawl together over her shoulders. 'Went and saw Doctor Jenkins a couple of weeks ago.'

'What did he say?'

'Cancer.' When she spoke, there wasn't even the slightest hint of self-pity in her tone.

Marric's pulse roared in his ears. Inwardly, he cursed himself for staying away from home for so long. Now there was no way to tell how much time his mother had left.

'Is there anything that can be done

— like surgery or something like that?' He was grasping at straws and he knew it.

Sarah shook her head. 'He doesn't think so.'

'Well, maybe we should see another sawbones. One of those big-city fellers, like they have up in Portland.'

Suddenly she looked very tired. 'No, Jack. I don't want to do that. I'm fifty-nine years old. I've had a good life. I don't want some doctor cutting me open, especially since there's no guarantee it would do any good.'

'I don't blame you,' said Marric, lowering his eyes.

The sound of an approaching horse pulled them both from their dark thoughts. Sarah Marric pushed back her chair and rose.

'I'll bet that's Marijo,' she said, her face brightening. 'She's been so excited to see you.'

Marric stood up and followed his mother down the short hallway into the living room. Through the front window he could see his sister slowing her mount near the front porch. He and his mother went out on to the porch to greet her.

'Hey there, little lady!' he called.

Marijo Marric alighted and rushed up the stairs to hug her brother. He squeezed her firmly and then held her back by the shoulders and looked her over.

'By God,' he said. 'My little sister's all grown up now.'

'I don't know about that!' she said, smiling widely.

It's true, though, he thought. *She has grown up.*

When he had left for California, she was still a skinny little colt. Now she had filled out, with the kind of shape that probably attracted a lot of attention among the men in Jasper. Like Marric, Marijo had pale green eyes; her light blonde hair was so pale as to be almost white, and it was pulled back in a pony tail at the back of her head. Her skin was fair, with a

41

sprinkling of freckles across her nose and under her eyes. Her straight white teeth gleamed as she smiled at him.

'I've been away too long,' he said.

'Yes, you have!' There was no anger in the young woman's voice.

'I just made some coffee,' said Sarah. 'Do you want some?'

'Of course.'

The trio returned to the kitchen and Marijo pulled her chair around the table to sit next to her brother. When her mother handed her a cup, she blew on it before taking a sip.

'So I heard tell that you're the schoolteacher here now,' Marric said. He looked at her with pride on his face.

'This is my first year,' she replied. 'I'm still learning.'

Sarah sat back down at the table. 'It's not an easy job!'

'No, it isn't,' Marijo agreed.

'Those kids giving you any trouble?' asked Marric playfully.

'A couple of them,' Marijo admitted. 'But I can handle them.'

'She can!' Sarah said.

Marric looked back and forth between his mother and his sister. They had always looked alike, but now the similarities were startling. He knew that Marijo had the same sort of quiet strength that their mother had demonstrated throughout their lives. Any unruly students would be whipped into shape very quickly.

'Marijo has more good news, too,' Sarah said.

'Oh, really? What's that?'

Marijo's face colored slightly. 'Well . . . ' she began.

'Don't tell me you're getting married!' Marric exclaimed.

'Yes, I am. I'm getting married.'

'To who? Is it someone I know?'

'Yes, you know him,' said Marijo, her face even more flushed now. 'It's Burt Kroll.'

'Burt Kroll?' Marric laughed, more in surprise than anything else. 'I would never have guessed that.'

Sarah said: 'You know, he's the

marshal of Jasper now.'

'He is?'

'Has been for — how long now, Marijo?'

'Almost four years.'

'I'll be damned,' Marric said. 'How long's he been courting you?'

'A little over a year.'

Marric hadn't thought of Burt Kroll in years. He remembered him clearly — a tall, muscular local boy, intelligent and good-natured. Burt's father worked at the mill where Floyd Marric was manager. When Marric had left Jasper, the younger Kroll had been working there, too. Now he was the law in the tiny village.

'How does Burt like being marshal?' he asked.

'He likes it quite a bit,' Marijo said. 'Jasper's a pretty quiet place, though. He hasn't been doing much shooting.'

Marric laughed. 'Good to hear.'

'He's coming over for supper tonight, Jack,' said Sarah. 'He's looking forward to seeing you.'

'That'll be nice.' He smothered a yawn, suddenly aware of his bone-deep exhaustion. 'When's Pa coming home?'

'He's going to try to leave early this afternoon,' said Sarah, looking at the clock on the wall above the wash basin. 'He said he'd try to get here by four.' She raised an eyebrow at her son. 'That gives you time to have a rest if you'd like. I know you must be real worn out after all those days on the trail.'

'I can't argue with that.'

Sarah put her hands on the table and pushed herself to her feet. 'Come on, then,' she said. 'I got your room ready.'

'I have to get back to the school-house,' Marijo said, patting her brother on the shoulder. 'I'll see you in a few hours.'

Marric hugged her again. 'Tell Burt to wear his Sunday finest.'

'I'll see to it,' she said with a laugh.

Marijo went out to the yard and rode away toward town. Marric fetched his saddle-bags and put his horse into the stable, brushing it and feeding it before going back in the house. He slept in his old bed, feeling more content than he had in years.

*　　*　　*

Always a punctual man, Floyd Marric arrived home at exactly four o'clock. He greeted his son warmly, and as Sarah finished preparing their meal the two men stood on the front porch and smoked cheroots.

The Marric patriarch had gained weight since the last time his son had seen him, but he still appeared remarkably vital. The only sign of the strain his wife's illness had taken on him was the latticework of wrinkles etched in the corners of his eyes. His face had a healthy ruddiness to it, and his thick dark hair showed only a few strands of silver.

'How long are you planning on staying, son?'

'I'm thinking I might stick around for

a good while. I don't want to leave Ma again.'

'She'll be happy to know you're not leaving.'

Marric stood leaning up against a rail on the veranda. 'Ma says she has good days and bad days,' he said.

Floyd removed his cheroot from his lips and examined the glowing ember at its tip. 'She keeps things from me,' he said. 'She doesn't want me to worry.'

'That's how she always was,' Marric observed.

'This has all happened so fast. She saw the doc. He said there's nothing to be done.'

'She seems to be taking it as well as could be expected.'

'That's your ma.'

* * *

Two horses drawing a buggy emerged from the forest, riding up the rutted trail to the house. Burt Kroll held the reins, and at his side was Marijo

Marric. Floyd waved in greeting as they pulled up before the veranda.

Kroll leapt down and walked around to help Marijo from the seat. He seemed a little nervous as he shook Marric's hand.

'It's been a long time, Jack,' he said. 'How's California been treating you?'

'I can't complain. I haven't made as much money as I'd hoped to, but that's all right.'

Floyd cleared his throat. 'Would you like a cheroot, Burt?'

'Yes, please.'

Marijo went in to assist her mother with the last preparations for supper. The men chatted for a few minutes before coming in to eat.

Jack Marric felt as if he had never left home, although he recognized how much things had changed. His mother now ill, apparently terminally, and his sister now betrothed. And yet coming home had felt perfectly natural, as if he had stepped back in time and picked up right where he had left off.

The evening passed pleasantly. Marijo invited her brother to a church social, and Marric reluctantly agreed to come. He found himself warming to the idea of having Burt Kroll in the family. He was a good man, honest and easy-going, and he clearly loved Marijo. The Krolls had been in the area for a long time; their roots in Jasper were, if anything, even deeper than those of the Marrics. With Burt as marshal and Marijo as the school teacher, the couple would hold two of the most important positions in town.

That night as he lay in his bed, Marric thought he would ask his father if any jobs were available at the mill. It looked like he was going to be home for a while, and he needed something to do with his time. He was eager to be working and paying his own way without having to deplete the savings he had brought with him from California. He decided that if he couldn't find work at the mill, he would try getting a job at one of the local ranches. He had many connections in ranching, and his reputation was unassailable. He drifted off to the sound of a steady rain pattering against the window of his room.

4

The lantern was turned down very low on the rough table at which Chet Harper was sitting. It had been a few hours since he had killed Marshal John Taylor and he didn't expect anyone to be on his trail yet, but he figured there was no use in attracting unwanted attention. Anyone riding past the cabin that he had shared with his late brothers in the forest south of Roseburg would have a hard time discerning the presence of anyone inside the rundown home.

Harper glanced across the darkened room to the bunk beds where Matt and Gil had slept. His own cot was against the other wall, near the wood stove. He found it difficult to accept that his brothers would never pass another night here, drinking and laughing as they usually did.

They had always been close, as anyone who had ever tried to come between them discovered. The brothers might fight amongst themselves, but they viewed the rest of the world as outsiders, and they always had each other's back when trouble came calling, as it frequently did. Like the times they had found girls and brought them home. Some of those girls had never left the shack alive, and sometimes that caused the law to come out, snooping around and asking questions. But the brothers had always kept their stories straight, and in every instance the law had backed down, unable to bring a case against them. It was almost like the Harpers were a law unto themselves.

They had had a lot of fun in this little shack, Chet thought. No one in Roseburg had the guts to go toe-to-toe with the Harpers. At least not until this stranger arrived a few nights ago . . .

He drained the last few drops of whiskey from his flask and screwed the cap back on. He slipped the flask back into the pocket of his coat and then froze suddenly when he heard the sound of foot-steps approaching in the darkness outside. After a moment, he reached down and palmed his Remington pistol.

A quiet voice spoke to him through the thin wall near the woodstove.

'Chet — you in there?'

Harper relaxed, but only slightly. 'Yeah,' he said. 'Come on in.'

The door creaked open and a figure stepped in and quickly closed it behind him. He was a small man, wearing tattered clothes. He reeked of alcohol.

'Ronnie, how are you?' asked Harper.

'Fine, fine,' Ronnie said. He was clearly uncomfortable being alone in the isolated shack with Chet Harper.

Harper's voice was smooth and reassuring. 'Did you get the information I asked for?'

Ronnie gulped. 'I was going to ask something . . . ' he said vaguely, unsure of what he was about to do.

'You got something to ask, go ahead and ask it.'

'Well, I was thinking, you know. Um, I'm really taking a big chance getting involved in all this.'

'I realize that, Ronnie. That's why I paid you.'

'Yeah — about that. Do you think you could give me a little more, seeing as how I could get in some big trouble for asking around like I did?'

Harper pulled at his beard, his eyes narrowing. 'I want the information first. If it's helpful, then I'll consider giving you some more cash.'

'Gee, thanks Chet.'

Harper made a dismissive gesture. 'Let's hear it.'

'Ralph Jackson was there at the saloon when your brothers were shot. He said he recognized the feller who did it.'

'How does he know him?'

'Said he lived in Jasper for a while when he was a kid. Went to school with the feller.'

'Jasper you say?'

'Yeah. You been there before?'

'Yep. I got an uncle who owns a ranch up there.' Harper rubbed his hands together. 'What's this gunslinger's name?'

'Marric,' Ronnie said. 'Jack Marric.'

'Marric,' Harper said, imprinting the name upon his mind. He seemed to be in a reverie for a moment. 'Did this . . . Marric feller recognize Ralph?'

Ronnie shook his head. 'I asked him that. He said he didn't think so. They only were in school together for a short time. He said he doubted Marric even knew who he was when they were kids.'

'And Marric's from Jasper?'

'Born and raised, according to Ralph.'

'Good, good.' Harper sighed heavily. 'It's time I moved on. There's nothing here for me anymore, now that Matt and Gil are dead. I ain't going to rest until I find this Marric and settle the score.'

'I don't blame you a bit, Chet,'

Ronnie said. He licked his lips expectantly. 'Now, about that money — '

'Oh, yes.' Harper rose. 'You did a good job, Ronnie.'

'Thanks.'

'Only thing is, how do I know you won't run your mouth?'

'Wh-what do you mean?'

'Did you tell Ralph you were asking on my behalf?'

'No.'

Harper smiled tightly. 'Good,' he said.

He reached into the right pocket of his coat and Ronnie smiled, holding out his hand, palm up. His smile evaporated when he saw Harper's hand emerge from his pocket with a derringer in it.

'Chet, please,' he said plaintively, his eyes bulging.

'Like I said, Ronnie — I have to know you won't run your mouth. And since your mouth is so damn big, there's only one way for me to rest easy.'

'I'll never tell anyone!'

Harper's lips spread into a malevolent smile. 'That's right — you'll never tell anyone.'

Ronnie opened his mouth to yell something, but the two rapid shots from the little gun robbed him of the power of speech. He collapsed sideways on to the dirt floor, and Chet Harper regarded his unmoving form for a moment before blowing out the lantern and stepping through the doorway into the darkness outside.

★ ★ ★

Jack Marric was sitting at the kitchen table, drinking a hot cup of coffee, when his father came down the hallway. It was only an hour after dawn, but Floyd Marric had always been an early riser, a trait he had passed on to his only son.

'Morning, boy,' Floyd said cheerfully. His face reflected the happiness he felt at having Jack at home again after so many years.

'Morning, Pa,' Marric replied. 'You want some coffee?'

'Hell yes, I do.'

Marric rose and poured coffee into a mug. He handed it to his father and sat back down.

'You know, I wanted to ask you something,' he said.

'What's that?' asked Floyd, blowing into his cup.

'I got a good chunk of money saved up, but I'd like to keep it that way. I think I need to get a job as quick as I can. You think there might be something for me at the mill?'

Floyd's bushy eyebrows drew together as he sat down at the table. 'You know, if you'd come back a year ago, I'd have had something for you. But right now we've got every position filled.' He sighed. 'Wish I could do something for you.'

Marric smiled reassuringly. 'Aw, it's no problem, Pa. There's always ranch work. Maybe I'll ride out to the Elson place and see if they've got any openings.'

Floyd nodded. 'They usually do. Old Howard's still running the place, even though he's past seventy. Works twice as hard as most of the young fellers out there.'

'He loved that ranch.'

'Still does! He'd be happy to see you, too. He always told me you were one of the best cowpunches he ever hired.'

Marric was now eager to ride out and talk to Howard Elson while it was still early. He spent a few more minutes chatting with his father, then rose from the table and put his cup in the wash basin.

'I'm going to go out there and have a talk with Howard,' he said, shrugging into his sheepskin. He placed his dun Stetson on his head. 'I'll be back early and spend some time with Ma. She mentioned some work that needed done on the roof of the shed.'

Floyd Marric laughed. 'She's been

riding me to take care of that for two weeks now, but I've been so damn busy.'

'Don't worry about it, Pa. It'll be done before you get home.'

Marric patted his father on the back and exited through the back door into the yard. He crossed to the stable and saddled his horse. Within five minutes, he was on the road, heading east away from Jasper. The McKenzie flowed to his right, sunlight glimmering off its rippled surface.

A feeling of contentment came over Jack Marric. When he had received the telegram about his mother's illness, he hadn't had any intention of returning to Jasper permanently. Even now it wasn't a firm decision in his mind. Yet something told him he would likely be staying for a long time — perhaps for good.

It was the little things that were moving him in that direction. The sight of the river, for example. How many days had he spent swimming in it, or fishing in it with his father for the night's supper? Countless.

The road he was travelling was so familiar to him that he felt as if he could close his eyes and find his way to any ranch or farm or logging camp within twenty miles. He laughed inwardly. He almost felt like a kid again. The only darkness on the horizon was the reality of his mother's declining health.

It took him twenty minutes before he reached the front gate to the Bar E ranch. The Elson family had owned it for forty years, gradually building it up from a small outfit into one of the largest ranches in this area of the Willamette Valley. Marric heeled his mount through the gate and started down the trail to the main house, a massive log structure that hadn't changed at all in his absence.

There were at least thirty men in the expansive pastures that bordered both sides of the trail. They regarded Marric briefly as he rode past, and then they returned to their work. He pulled leather near the barn, dismounting and tying his reins over the hitching post. He could hear men's voices coming from the cook shack behind the barn. He walked around the corner, making his way toward the cook shack. The aroma of bacon and coffee wafted across the crisp morning air and filled his nostrils.

Marric was about ten feet away from the door when two men emerged from inside. They were laughing about something when they spotted Marric. The man on the right stopped dead in his tracks, and the other man took a few more steps before he, too, halted.

'I'll be goddamned,' said the first man. 'It's Jack Marric.'

He was tall and rawboned, with a thick beard that came to a point below his chin. He wore range clothes, but they were exceptionally clean and tidy. His dark eyes inspected Marric with contempt.

'Chance Elson,' Marric replied. 'It's

been a long time. Last I heard you were somewhere in Wyoming.'

'Yeah, I was. Last I heard you were panning for gold down in California.'

'That's right. Got back yesterday.'

'What the hell you doing at the Bar E?'

'Thought I might have a word with your pa about getting a job out here.'

Elson snorted disdainfully. 'Christ Almighty — we wouldn't give you a job if you was the last cow hand in Oregon.'

The hostility that suffused Chance Elson's every word didn't surprise Marric. The two men were almost exactly the same age, and they had known each other from babyhood. They had never been friends, for their personalities were far too disparate for that. Elson was the son of a rich landowner; he had always looked down on Marric, whose family wasn't poor by any means, but admittedly possessed nothing near to the money and influence of the Elsons. There had been an element of competition between the two young men from a very early age. However, there was a depth of anger, laced with potential violence, in Elson's words and manner that Marric hadn't anticipated.

Suddenly he realized why. It all came back to him now — the brief period, seven years previous, when he had had a brief romance with Holly Shay. It was the only explanation for Elson's rage.

'Be damned, Chance — you're not still sore about Holly Shay, are you?'

Elson clenched his jaw and a vein throbbed in his left temple.

'You bet your ass I'm sore about Holly. I got every reason to be.'

Without thinking, Marric laughed. He shook his head in amused wonder.

'Hell, Chance! You got to move forward with your life instead of mewling over some girl you ain't seen in years.'

By the time, nearly a dozen men had emerged from the cook shack. They stood gathered behind Elson in a loose half-circle. Marric looked them over but didn't recognize a single one of them.

'Don't you tell me what I should or shouldn't do,' Elson snapped, suddenly conscious of the crowd that now observed the scene. 'You played around with the wrong man, Marric.'

Jack Marric could feel a rising tide of anger within himself, but he hadn't ridden out here to get into a fight. He knew he should just turn around and ride back home. There was no point in escalating this conflict. Still, there was something about Chance Elson that got under his skin. It had been many years since he had even thought of the man, but he was now getting a vivid reminder of just how irritating he was. The fact that Elson was clearly putting on some sort of show for the men who worked for him only further annoyed Marric.

Almost despite himself, he decided to twist the knife a little.

'I never pursued Holly,' he said. 'She pursued me. I didn't even know you were courting her at the time.'

'Like hell you didn't!' Elson said, shrillness rising in his voice.

The expression on Marric's face was now almost pitying.

'She never mentioned it, actually,' he said. 'Funny, ain't it?'

'Goddamn you!' Elson exclaimed, moving forward and lowering his hand toward the pistol in his holster.

The man who had walked out of the cook shack with him intervened, reaching out and gripping Elson's arm firmly.

'Hold it, Chance,' he said. 'Your pa's going to be back in a week. You know what he'd do if he found out you were in a gunfight, right here on his land? He'd skin you alive.'

Elson jerked his arm out of the man's grasp and glared at him. But he was now careful to keep his hand away from his pistol.

'Listen to the man, Chance,' Marric said. 'One more second and I'd have killed you where you stand. You've never been fast with a pistol.' All the amusement had left Marric's tone. He was now deadly serious.

One of the men behind Elson chortled at Marric's words. Elson pivoted, his eyes blazing.

'Who did that?' he demanded. 'Who, damn it?!'

The men avoided his glance, careful not to provoke him. Elson turned back toward Marric, at whom he stared for several seconds, wondering how to save face in front of the ranch hands he made a habit of bullying and dominating. He knew he couldn't outdraw Jack Marric; indeed, there were few people who could, apart from professional gunslingers. But what Chance Elson lacked in gun skills he more than made up for when it came to his fists. He knew what he had to do.

Elson unbuckled his gun belt and dropped it into the grass at his feet. He began to roll up his sleeves.

'You think you're mighty big with that Colt,' he said. 'I'll bet I can beat your ass into the dirt — right here, right now.'

Marric returned Elson's glare. Then he, too, removed his gun belt, folding it carefully and laying it on top of a nearby woodpile. He placed his Stetson beside the belt, then rolled up his sleeves.

Cracking his knuckles, he grinned at Elson.

'Let's do this,' he said.

5

Fists up, Jack Marric and Chance Elson moved in on each other.

Marric sized up his opponent. Elson was the same size, strong and with good speed. In earlier years, he had also demonstrated an ability to take a punch. Marric thought he detected a certain wariness in Elson, as if the presence of the spectators had pushed the man into a fight that he hadn't really wanted. Marric hoped this was the case, as it might offer an advantage.

Just as Marric had this thought, Elson stepped in close and sent a hard right jab at his opponent's head. Marric pulled back quickly and the blow barely connected, but it seemed to embolden Elson, who followed it up with an uppercut that came within a centimeter of connecting.

The bastard hits hard, Marric thought.

He wants to finish this quick.

The realization only confirmed Marric's hunch about the fear in Chance Elson. He was thankful that he had been quick on his feet, because either of Elson's punches would have done damage had they connected fully.

'You look scared, Marric,' Elson said, clearly frustrated.

Marric didn't respond. Instead, he took Elson's approach and moved in close. He feinted with his left and then struck hard with his right. Rather than punch Elson, though, he backhanded him across the mouth, splitting the man's lip. Blood burst from Elson's mouth and dripped down the front of his nicely pressed shirt.

Startled, Elson touched his fingers to his lips and examined the blood that continued to pour from them.

'Before I put you to sleep, I thought you deserved to be slapped,' Marric explained. 'I won't be so nice next time.'

Over Elson's shoulder, a few of the

watching men smirked or smothered chuckles. Marric knew there was nothing more offensive to Elson than being mocked in front of those he considered his inferiors.

Fury surged within Elson. He lunged toward Marric, wrapping his arms around the man's torso, and hurled him backward. Marric tumbled on to the ground with Elson on top of him. The wind had been knocked out of Marric, and he gasped as he struggled to get a breath.

Elson's fists smashed into Marric's head. Marric swung a left that miraculously connected with Elson's jaw, but it appeared to have no effect. Marric brought his arms up to cover his head, suddenly worried that he would lose consciousness if he were unable to deflect the blows that rained down upon him.

'Who's laughing now, huh?' shouted Elson. He saw victory within his grasp, and its closeness exhilarated him.

Marric was now absorbing most of

the punches on his arms, thwarting Elson's attack. The latter leapt to his feet in exasperation, deciding to kick the fallen man. Although his head was spinning, Marric recognized the opening. Like a striking cobra, he kicked Elson in the shins with all the force he could muster. Elson's legs were swept out from under him and he hurtled forward, slamming into the ground face first. Marric's maneuver had been executed so quickly that Elson hadn't even had time to put out his hands; his face took the full impact.

A murmur ran through spectators, and it grew in volume and intensity when, after several seconds, Elson was finally able to roll himself over on to his back, exposing his face to the men of the Bar E.

His nose was bent at a grotesque angle, and his upper lip had now split widely, exposing the bloodied gums beneath it. Four or five of his upper teeth were gone, and a few others were crooked or dangling by the roots. His face was covered in dirt and blood. A pinkish fluid was filling his left eye.

Marric had managed to get back on his feet. He looked down at the man before him with disgust.

'I think you've had enough, Chance,' he said, his breathing labored.

Elson wasn't entirely coherent when he spoke. The totality of his humiliation seemed beyond his ability to comprehend.

'I — I . . . ' he began, struggling to find the words. 'I'll kill you!' He spat into the dirt, a trickle of blood and saliva streaming from his mutilated mouth.

'You should probably help him up,' Marric said to the man who had emerged from the shack with Elson. 'What's your name?'

'Hunter,' said the man. 'Doyle Hunter.'

'Fine — you better take him in the house, Doyle Hunter,' Marric said evenly. 'Don't give him that gun belt or he might try something stupid. His pa will hang you from the nearest tree if I have to kill him.' Doyle Hunter hesitated. Elson tried to push himself to his feet, but he only managed to make it to his knees before he fell sideways back on to the ground. The man was clearly done fighting, whether he liked it or not.

Hunter walked forward and leaned down to help Elson. He got the man halfway up before the latter fell down once more.

'Goddamn, boys — one of you get over here and give me a hand!' he exclaimed, and immediately two men broke from the half-circle of onlookers and assisted Hunter. One of the men took Elson's feet while the other helped Hunter with the arms; together, they moved the bloodied and defeated rancher toward the main house.

Jack Marric had strapped his gunbelt back around his waist. He secured the thin strip of leather at the bottom of the holster, tying it firmly to his thigh. He placed his feet apart and scrutinized the remaining Bar E men.

'Now I'm going to ride out of here,' he said. 'Any of you want to pick up where Chance left off? If you do, keep in mind that I'm fighting with pistols from now on.'

The men largely avoided his intense gaze. A few locked eyes with Marric, then quickly looked away. Only a small but powerfully built man defiantly glared back. He had prematurely grey hair, slicked back with some sort of grease. A large pistol bulged in the holster at his side; it was a Navy Colt, just like Marric's.

'How about you, feller?' Marric said with a sneer. 'You look like you want to say something.'

The small man didn't flinch. 'I got a lot to say. But I'll say it when I'm good and ready. I ain't going to cause more trouble for Chance.'

'That's mighty sagacious of you, pard,' said Marric. 'Maybe we'll meet again and you can tell me what's on your mind.'

'Oh, we'll meet again. Ain't no question about that.'

Marric smiled. 'I'll be looking forward to it,' he said.

His right hand dangling near his holster, he walked backward several paces until he came to the edge of the barn. Here he pivoted and walked around the front of the building to the post where he had left his horse. He put a foot in a stirrup and mounted, looking in the direction from which he had come to see if anyone was following him. No one was. He neck-reined his mount and touched spurs to its flanks, heading up the trail toward the gate of the Bar E. When he reached the road beyond, he turned right and rode back toward Jasper.

*   *   *

Doyle Hunter stood in the shade on the veranda of the Bar E's main house. His gaze was directed to the gate. A small elderly man had just passed through it and was riding toward the house. He wore black clothes and a rumpled black derby. He made his way toward the house at a leisurely pace, then alighted at the bottom of the steps.

'Howdy, Doyle,' the man said, opening a saddle-bag and removing a battered leather valise. 'Chance inside?'

Harper nodded, his face drawn. 'He's on the couch in the parlor, doc. He's going to need a lot of stitches.'

The doctor climbed the steps and walked past Hunter into the house. Hunter removed his pipe from his pocket and filled it from a sack of tobacco. He struck a match and stirred it over the bowl, puffing gently as he did so. When he had the pipe going nicely, he tossed the match into the mud that bordered the veranda.

What a mess, he thought. *Chance and his damn big mouth.*

He took the pipe from between his teeth and sat down in a wicker chair. He had been the foreman at the Bar E for nearly four years. The first two years had been ideal, but the last two had been seriously marred by the return of Chance Elson. Chance's father had told Hunter that he would be expected to keep an eye on Chance, whose hot temper and impulsive actions had gotten him into trouble many times over the years. This included a scrape in Wyoming over a judge's daughter; it had cost Howard Elson a pretty penny to extract his son from that debacle.

And now this.

Hunter knew that Howard Elson would be furious when he returned from Medford, where he was negotiating with some cattle agents. He also knew that the old man's anger would only briefly be directed at the foreman; he would quickly shift his disapproval to his son, who had been a thorough disappointment since boyhood.

The dilemma that now confronted Hunter was how to take care of the problem posed by Jack Marric. Although Marric hadn't been home to Jasper in years, he was still a widely known figure in the area. Hunter had heard of him and his reputation as a skilled gunman and superbly knowledgeable ranch hand. Hunter knew that as soon as Chance Elson recovered, he would seek revenge on Marric. Judging from what had taken place that morning, there was a better than good chance that Marric would kill him. It was up to Doyle Hunter to see that that never happened. If it did, the results would be devastating for the men who worked the Bar E, particularly its foreman.

The door to the bunkhouse creaked on its hinges, drawing Hunter's attention. He watched impassively as the short, grey-haired young cowboy came toward him. The man's name was Bill Golding, and there wasn't a thing about him that Hunter liked apart from his skill as a cowpunch. Golding's expression was cocky as he crossed the yard and then walked up the veranda steps.

'Sawbones get here yet?' asked Golding.

'A few minutes ago.'

Golding shook his head with mock sympathy. 'I sure wouldn't want to have to break the news to the old man,' he said. 'He's going to be awful mad.'

Hunter's face was impassive. 'That he is,' he said simply, wondering what was on Golding's mind. He hadn't seen the earlier conversation between Marric and Golding.

'I was thinking . . . ' Golding said tentatively.

'Yeah?'

'Yeah.'

'What about?'

'That Jack Marric really thinks he's something, don't he?'

'Well, he seems like the type who backs up his words. That's more than I can say for a lot of fellers I've met in my time.'

Golding frowned, not sure if Hunter's words were directed at him. 'I don't like him one bit. That wasn't a fair fight, if you ask me.'

'Hmmm.'

'What do you think?' asked Golding, squinting at Hunter out of the corner of his eye.

'I think maybe Chance bit off more than he could chew,' Hunter asserted. 'He's been known to do that, in case you haven't noticed.'

'Still, it don't sit right with me. I think maybe someone should teach Marric a lesson.'

Hunter shifted in his chair. He wondered if Bill Golding wasn't offering him precisely the solution he sought to the problem of Jack Marric. Golding wasn't much with his fists, but he was easily the fastest draw at the Bar E, having won every shooting contest in the Jasper area over the course of the last couple years. Despite Marric's reputation for gunplay, Hunter was confident that Golding could hold his own in the right circumstances.

'You think you could take Marric?' he asked.

'Hell, I could do it standing on my

head,' Golding said. 'All I need is the chance.'

Hunter regarded Golding curiously before speaking again.

'What do you have in mind, Bill?'

6

The sky was mostly dark when Marric and his sister arrived at the First Presbyterian Church of Jasper. They had ridden in the little two-person buggy that Floyd Marric had bought nearly twenty years before. Marric parked behind the livery and set the brake. It was only a few yards from the church.

The church held such informal gatherings once every few months. Most of the townspeople attended, along with their children.

The front steps were crowded with people waiting to get in. Burt Kroll greeted Marijo and escorted her inside as Marric exchanged greetings with various old friends and acquaintances who were notably happy to see him again after so many years. A few asked about his mother's health. Nearly ten minutes passed before Marric was able to make his way into the church.

The pews had been moved aside to make room for dancing. There were ribbons and large bows hanging on the wall at various locations, adding to the festive atmosphere. At the front of the room were three musicians — a cellist, a fiddler, and a banjo player. Marric thought they must have come from Eugene; musicians were awfully scarce in these parts.

He saw Kroll and Marijo sipping punch and talking to an elderly couple. He removed his hat and joined them.

'By golly, it's Jack!' said the old man, a smile spreading across his face. Marric recognized him as Clem McCarthy, a manager at the mill. They shook hands.

'How you doing, Clem?' Marric asked. He nodded at Mrs. McCarthy. 'Good to see you, ma'am.'

'What do you think about your sister marrying this feller?' she asked, nudging Kroll playfully.

'I can't complain about her choice. He might lock me up if I do.'

They continued their friendly chat, and soon the church was full. The first song began, and Marric was pleasantly surprised to find that the musical standards were much higher than he had expected. Several more people came to greet him, and twice he was asked to dance.

Marric realized he was thirsty. He made his way to the back of the room and refilled his cup with punch. As he replaced the dipper in the punch bowl, the back door of the church opened and he raised his eyes to see Bill Golding enter, accompanied by two other Bar E men whose faces he recognized but whose names he didn't know.

Gazes locked, Marric and Golding stared at each other for several seconds before either spoke.

'Look what we have here,' Golding said, nudging his companions. 'If it ain't Jack Marric.' Golding's tone was aggressive but tense. Marric smirked, amused by the little man before him.

'Well, if ain't the best-dressed bantam rooster in Jasper,' he retorted. 'You here looking for a game hen?'

Golding's face colored. 'You're a funny feller, ain't you, Marric? I think someone needs to wipe that smile off your face.'

'Chance Elson thought the same thing. How'd that work out for him?'

'Chance ain't done with you. You picked the wrong fight. The Elsons got a lot of friends around here.'

'I've known the Elsons since you were a suckling.'

'Then you should have known better than to — '

'I think I've heard about enough from you,' Marric said. The little man was starting to get under his skin. 'How about we stop jawing and have a talk outside. You can bring your friends if you want.'

Marric turned as Kroll finished up a waltz with Marijo. The marshal had noticed the arrival of the three new-comers, and after he escorted Marijo to a chair he came over to where Marric was standing.

'Everything all right over here, fellers?' he inquired.

'You hear what he did to Chance Elson?' Golding asked, pointing toward Marric. 'Sawbones says Chance's jaw might be broken. He swallowed quite a few teeth, too.'

'From what I heard, Chance brought that on himself,' said Kroll, his face set in harsh lines.

'That's a lie!' Golding exclaimed. Several heads among the crowd turned toward him. 'He was going to pull a gun on Chance.'

Kroll shrugged. 'Chance is a big boy. He shouldn't start things he can't finish.'

'So you're taking his side? Why — because you think you're going to marry his sister?'

'What did you say?' Kroll asked in a low voice. An element of danger had entered the conversation.

'I, uh, well — ' muttered Golding, who was aware of having crossed a line with the marshal.

'I don't care who your boss is, Golding,' Kroll continued. 'You've got a big mouth. That can get you in trouble if you're not careful.' He paused. 'A whole lot of trouble.'

Golding's face reddened and he seemed ready to say something, but thought better of it. He hitched his pants and walked around the edge of the table, followed by the other men. They, too, cast hostile glances at Jack Marric, who watched them with disinterest.

'I spotted those fellers right when they came in,' Kroll said quietly. 'They don't usually come to church socials.'

'Maybe they're wanting to learn about Jesus.'

Kroll grinned. 'Not likely.'

'What're their names?' Marric asked, sipping his punch.

'Little feller is Bill Golding. He's

been around for a few years, working for the Elsons. He's got a bad reputation. Only time he usually comes into town is to get drunk at the saloon.'

'Seems like he's got something to prove.'

'That's about right, I reckon.'

'He a good pard of Chance Elson's?'

'He'd like to be. I don't think Chance pays him much mind.'

'Maybe he's looking for a promotion.'

Marric and Kroll watched as Golding talked to a young woman on the far side of the room. Her lack of interest was evident, but Golding seemed unperturbed. At one point, he laughed loudly at one of his own jokes.

'Doesn't look like he's having much luck,' Kroll noted.

'Who are the other two?' Marric asked.

'Tim Campbell and Hal Clement,' Kroll said. 'They've only been around for a few months. They spend a lot of time in the saloon, too.'

The trio of musicians struck up another tune and the floor soon filled with dancers. Marric noticed that Golding had been unable to entice the young lady to dance with him. He was now huddled in the corner with Campbell and Clement. They were passing a flask between them. Marijo approached and put her arm through Kroll's.

'What are you two talking about? You both look so serious.'

Kroll nodded toward the three men, who had now nearly polished off the contents of the flask.

'Bill Golding and his two pals over there,' he said.

Marijo looked briefly where he had indicated. 'I've seen them around a time or two. One of them was drunk in the mercantile a few weeks ago. When Leo asked him to leave, I almost thought he was going to hit him. Imagine that — hitting a man more than twice your age.'

'Wish I'd been there,' Kroll

remarked. 'I'd have escorted him out personally.'

'It was disgusting,' Marijo added.

Marric glanced at his sister. 'You two sitting this one out?'

'Let's get back out there,' Kroll said with a smile.

He escorted Marijo out to the floor and they began to dance. Marric watched them for a few minutes, then decided to step outside for a smoke. The cold night air was invigorating as he stood on the back stairs. He could smell the river, which burbled softly about a dozen yards from where was standing.

He fingered the makings from his pocket and rolled a cigarette. As he smoked, he regarded the moon, which shone brightly above the trees in the night sky. He thought of his mother and her quiet strength. He knew she was happy to have him back and, although he couldn't restore her health, he was pleased to make her days a little more bearable.

Marric rolled another cigarette and removed the watch from the inside pocket of his sheepskin. It was after ten o'clock now. Soon the dance would be over.

He had just completed that thought when Burt Kroll came out of the church.

'They're winding things down in there,' he said. 'Banjo player's pretty drunk.'

Marric laughed. 'I'll help put the chairs away,' he said.

He dropped his cigarette on to the step and crushed the embers under the tip of his boot. Kroll held the door open for him and they both went back in. When he looked around the room, he noticed that Golding, Campbell, and Clement were nowhere in sight. The front doors were propped open and much of the crowd had already made its way out front to the waiting horses, carriages, and wagons. Ten or twelve men were still inside, moving the pews and tables under the stern direction of the minister's wife.

Twenty minutes later, the room was organized to her satisfaction. Marijo was waiting on the front stoop of the church when Kroll and Marric emerged. She was talking to a middle-aged woman whose son was one of Marijo's students.

'He really is making progress,' Marijo said reassuringly. 'He's almost caught up to the others in arithmetic.'

The woman beamed at Marijo's words, and Marric realized how suited his sister was for her chosen profession. He wasn't in the least surprised. She had spoken of becoming a teacher from a very early age. He was proud to think of the contribution she was making to the town where she had been born and raised.

The women concluded their conversation and Marijo turned to Kroll and Marric. There were no other people remaining from the dance.

'Everything taken care of in there?' she asked.

Kroll nodded. 'Mrs Jones runs a tight ship,' he said. 'I don't know how the reverend keeps up with her.'

'I don't envy him a bit,' Marric said drily. 'I don't think she's ever smiled in her life.'

'Me neither,' Kroll said.

'Don't be too hard on her,' Marijo advised. 'He's not exactly a prize himself.'

Kroll yawned loudly. 'I better be going. You two should, too. You both got to get up early.'

Marric and his sister agreed, and Kroll helped her down the steps to Jasper's Main Street. He helped Marijo up into her seat as Marric climbed up and took the reins in his hands.

'I hope to see you tomorrow,' Marijo said to the marshal.

'Me, too,' Kroll said, patting her hand.

Marric waved and shook the reins. The two horses moved forward, their hoofs making squishing noises in the thick mud. A few hundred yards down the road, they turned a corner and vanished from Kroll's view.

The marshal turned and walked in the opposite direction. The street was in darkness, the only light coming from a few lamps on the plank sidewalk up ahead. He climbed the stairs in front of Jasper's only saloon and peered over the batwings. Three men were inside, including the barkeep, who raised a hand toward Kroll. Kroll grinned and waved, then continued down the block, past the post office, the hardware store, and the café. Apart from the stragglers in the saloon, the tiny business district had been abandoned for the night. Jasper was completely quiet.

The combined law office and jail was situated between the café and the blacksmith's shed. Kroll's quarters were on the second floor, accessible by a staircase from the small walkway on the side.

He yawned loudly as he climbed the stairs, his tired mind occupied by thoughts of Marijo Marric. Those thoughts were dispelled abruptly when he reached the landing. He drew his pistol and pulled back the hammer, his eyes riveted on the smashed doorway. The door had been kicked in and was hanging crookedly on its hinges.

A frigid breeze blew past him, raising the hairs on the back of his neck. He leaned forward, casting a cautious glance into the room. He could only make out the area near the door, and no one stirred in the shadows there.

Kroll wondered if someone had burgled his quarters. A few months before he had arrested two of the local boys for breaking into the general store. He found the idea of being robbed mildly amusing. The burglar would be very disappointed if he were looking for anything interesting or valuable there, for the lawman lived a spartan existence.

'Anybody in there?' Kroll called into the room. 'If you are, just come out. I've got my pistol here. No need to do anything stupid.'

Nearly a minute passed before Kroll decided to go in. He moved into the doorway and crouched, his pistol raised. He could see very little in the murky shadows. He rose and fished a match from a pocket, making his way to the table beside his bed. He replaced his pistol in the holster and lighted the lantern. He turned to see what could be done about the door.

As he did so, the double doors of the big oaken wardrobe burst open. A man leapt toward him, smashing the barrel of his pistol against the marshal's head before Kroll had time to respond.

Blinding light burst through Kroll's skull and he fell backward, crashing against a small desk. Someone drew his pistol from his holster and he heard it clatter across the floor. He saw the lantern light glimmer off the gun barrel as his attacker raised his pistol again, and he raised his arm to protect himself. Pain shot through his forearm as the gun smashed into it. Kroll slammed his shoulder against the man, sending him sprawling. Suddenly he recognized him as Hal Clement.

Clement was back on his feet almost instantly, his face contorted with rage.

'You son of a bitch,' he said, almost spitting the words at Kroll. He had managed to keep a grip on his gun, and he leveled it now at the marshal's chest.

'Stop!' called a voice from the doorway. Both men turned their heads and saw Bill Golding step into the room. Behind him lurked the much larger figure of Tim Campbell. 'Don't shoot him, you moron. You'll wake half the town.'

'What the hell do you think you're doing, Golding?' Kroll asked.

'We were going to take care of that smart ass, Jack Marric,' Golding explained. 'But we didn't want his sister mixed up in all this.' He leered. 'She's a nice lady, ain't she?'

Despite his small stature, the man was obviously the leader of the three Bar E cowpunchers. There was an animalistic intensity about him, an undercurrent of aggression that enabled him to dominate the others. Before he had only seemed like a cocky trouble-maker, but now Kroll looked at Golding and knew he was in the presence of a stone-cold killer.

'If you stop now, a jury might not hang you,' Kroll said. 'You're playing for big stakes here, Bill.'

'Shut the hell up!' Golding spat. He looked at Clement and Campbell. 'Let's tie him up, boys. He'll be easier to move that way.'

Campbell stepped forward and grabbed at Kroll's sleeve. Kroll didn't wait for him to get a better grip. He thrust his elbow into Campbell's face, and when Golding tried to intervene, Kroll drove his boot savagely into the man's crotch. Golding yelped and bent forward, his slicked-back grey hair shining in the light.

Campbell's fist shot out, taking Kroll in the chin. Pure adrenaline kept the marshal on his feet. He grasped the front of Campbell's shirt and pulled the man toward him. He could see Clement regaining his feet and he wanted to take out Campbell before Clement rejoined the fight. He head-butted Campbell and the man groaned, trying to disentangle himself.

Clement was only a few feet from the grappling men. Kroll pulled Campbell by the shirt, tearing the fabric and sending buttons flying, and maneuvered him into Clement's path. With all the strength he could muster, he shoved Campbell toward Clement, releasing the man's shirt. Campbell's weight sent both men toppling over.

Kroll hesitated for a moment, not sure whether he should try to fetch his gun from the floor by the bed or simply make a run for it through the open doorway. He concluded that his best chance for survival was to exit the room.

He had almost forgotten about the presence of Bill Golding, who now leapt into his path and drove a hand toward Kroll's abdomen. Kroll grunted, shocked by the power of Golding's punch. Then a strange sensation shot through his belly, and he looked down. The bloody handle of a knife protruded from his navel. Golding had stepped back, an evil smile on his face. Kroll blinked a few times, then put both hands around the knife handle and pulled.

The blade was at least six inches long. It was also extremely sharp — the sort of weapon a violent man keeps close just in case there is killing to be done.

'It's like a razor, ain't it, Marshal?' Golding asked with a threadbare chuckle.

He moved forward to take the knife from Kroll's hands. Blood was oozing down the lawman's pants and soaking his boots. He swayed on his feet but didn't go down. Golding tried to clutch the handle. Kroll tightened his fingers around it, and the blade arced fleetingly in the lamplight.

Golding shrieked, his hands darting

up to his face. A deep, vicious cut ran from the corner of his right eye, gouging through his nose and carving a line across the lower part of his left cheek to the jawline. He tripped over his own feet and hit the floor with a thud, rolling into a fetal position and sobbing in agony.

Burt Kroll was unsteady as he turned to face Campbell and Clement. The last thing he saw was a chair descending toward his head, and then darkness engulfed him and he saw nothing more.

7

Jack Marric was standing on the front porch of the family home, drinking coffee with his father, when he saw the three men emerge from the forest at the far end of the yard. He recognized them instantly as Elmer Smith, the mayor of Jasper, and Carl and Gordon Jeffers, the brothers who co-owned the hardware store. The Jefferses were members of the town council. All of the men's faces were grim as they approached the house.

Floyd Marric set his cup down on the small table near the front door.

'Those fellers look serious,' he said. 'I wonder what's going on.'

'Me, too,' said Marric warily.

The men halted near the porch and exchanged terse greetings with the Marrics.

'What can I do for you, gents?' asked Floyd.

'We've got some bad news, I'm afraid,' said the mayor. 'Burt Kroll's been murdered.'

'By God,' said Floyd. 'How?'

'Somebody beat him to death in his room over the jail last night.'

Marric's eyes glinted as he flicked the rest of his coffee out of the cup on to the grass. 'I know exactly who did it, mayor,' he said, his voice tight.

'Who, Jack?'

'Bill Golding, along with two other fellers from the Bar E.'

Carl Jeffers frowned. 'You sure about that?'

Marric nodded slowly. 'I'm sure. They tried to start a fight at the church dance last night over some trouble I had with Chance Elson. Burt stepped in and shut them down. They're the only ones who would do this.'

'You sure it wasn't Golding by himself?' asked Smith.

Marric's faint smile was mirthless. 'He couldn't have handled Burt Kroll by himself, especially if there weren't any gunplay. No — the others helped him. You can be sure of that.'

The door opened behind them and Marijo emerged, her face worried.

'Good morning, gentlemen,' she said. 'Is there anything wrong?'

The men removed their hats and exchanged glances, unsure about what to say. Then Floyd Marric cleared his throat and touched his daughter's elbow.

'Honey, come on inside with me. We need to talk.'

Her chin seemed to tremble for a moment, and then she regained her full composure.

'All right, Pa,' she said, and they went into the house, the door closing behind them.

Marric turned back to the men in the yard. 'Someone's going to have to arrest those fellers,' he asserted. 'This is cold-blooded murder, plain and simple. I don't know why they attacked Burt, because I'm sure it's me they would have liked to get their hands on. But there's no doubt about who did this.'

Mayor Smith folded his hands over his saddle-horn. 'That's something else we wanted to talk to you about, Jack.'

'Yes — what's that?'

Smith glanced down, forming his words, then raised his eyes again to meet Marric's gaze. 'We wanted to ask if you would be willing to take Burt's place as the town marshal here in Jasper — at least on a temporary basis.'

Marric's eyebrows lifted. 'You serious?'

'He's serious, Jack,' said Gordon Jeffers. 'We're all serious. We haven't had a murder in Jasper in eleven years. For someone to do this to our marshal, particularly to a feller like Burt, it's just — well, it won't stand.'

'Doesn't the sheriff have a deputy he can send out here?'

The mayor shook his head. 'He can't spare a single man at the moment. Believe me — I thought of that. We need someone who can do something like this without backing down. This ain't going to be a little job, taking these men into custody. We need someone who can handle himself.'

'What makes you think that's me?'

'We heard what happened out at the Bar E,' said Smith. 'You went up against Chance Elson on his own ranch, in front of his own men. And you licked him good. That's why Golding and these others fellers — by the way, did you get their names?'

'Hal Clement and Jack Campbell.'

'All right, that's why Golding, Clement, and Campbell came after you. They did it for Chance. I don't know if he sent them, but they were trying to get back at you for humiliating him like you did.'

Marric sighed. 'Look, I'd like to help, but taking over as marshal — I just don't know about that. I've never worn a badge in my life.'

'It's just temporary,' said the mayor, raising a placating hand. 'You get those three in the jail, and we'll see about

107

finding someone to take on the job full-time.'

Marric rolled his shoulders, looking thoughtfully past the men toward the misty, forested ridges beyond. He hadn't even had time to come to grips with Burt Kroll's death, and already he was being pulled in an entirely new, and very dangerous, direction.

Me with a badge? he thought. *Ridiculous!*

But as he looked out at the landscape of his home, the little town where good, hardworking, honest people did their best to make a living and feed their families, he knew what choice he would make. Jasper had been lucky to have a man like Burt Kroll as its marshal — a decent man who believed in the law, and who wasn't afraid to stick his neck out if that was what it took to do the right thing.

And now Burt was dead — beaten to death, no less, by three lowdown cowards, none of whom would have faced the marshal one-on-one. The image of Kroll's dead body flashed across Marric's mind, and he shuddered inwardly. Kroll was a big man, and very tough. He wouldn't have gone down easily. Whoever had found the marshal that morning had surely discovered a scene of horror.

The piercing cry of his sister from inside the house jarred Marric from his contemplation.

'No!' she screamed. 'Pa, it can't be! Oh, Lord — Burt!'

Marric heard his parents speaking in consoling tones, trying somehow to comfort their daughter. Her dreams, her future, the man she was to marry — all those things had been snatched from her in the darkness of the night.

'I'll take the job,' Marric said, his jaw jutting resolutely. 'I'll take over as marshal.'

'You will?' Smith asked, his face lighting up. 'You will!'

'Yes. Let me get my gun and saddle up.' Marric turned, and then paused. 'Thing is, though — I think I'm going to need a deputy. At least when I head out to the Bar E. No telling what they got waiting for me out there.'

'You can take me,' said Gordon Jeffers. 'I got my pistol and my Winchester. I ain't afraid to use them.'

Marric was surprised, but as he looked at the younger of the two Jeffers brothers, he realized the man would likely make a fine deputy. He was a big man, somewhere in his early forties, with clear blue eyes and a laconic disposition. He wasn't the sort of man who would panic in a fight, although his skills with a gun were probably lacking.

'I'd be glad to have you along, Gordon,' Marric said. 'Much obliged.'

The mayor opened his coat and removed a shiny star from inside. He held it out to Jack Marric.

'This was Burt's,' he explained. 'I know he'd be proud to have you wear it.'

Marric took the badge, looking at it with just a tinge of disbelief. Then he pinned it on to his shirt and put a hand on the doorknob.

'I'll be right back,' he said. He glanced at Gordon Jeffers. 'Then we can head straight out to the Bar E.'

'I'm ready whenever you are, Marshal,' said Jeffers.

Marric disappeared into the house and then came back out within two minutes. He had strapped on his gunbelt and donned his sheepskin and Stetson. As he closed the door behind him, Carl Jeffers asked: 'How's Miss Marijo doing?'

'Not good,' Marric replied.

The pain his sister was experiencing only fueled his anger at the three Bar E men, and toward Chance Elson, whose foolish bravado had started the entire conflict. He wondered if it really had been Chance who had sent those men to the church the night before. It would be something to discuss when he and Gordon Jeffers arrived at the Bar E.

'I'll get my horse,' he said, stepping down into the yard and crossing over to the stable. Presently he returned, leading his chestnut by the reins. He put a foot in a stirrup and climbed into leather. The four men rode down the trail through the woods to the main road. To the west was Jasper; to the east, the Bar E.

'We'll be heading back to town, then,' Mayor Smith said. 'Just so you know, the whole town council got together this morning before we three rode out here. They voted unanimously to grant you all the legal powers as town marshal of Jasper. I thought you might like to know that in case Elson or his boys try to say you don't have the authority to arrest anyone.'

'Thanks for that tidbit, Mayor. I'll keep it in mind.'

Mayor Smith and Carl Jeffers rode away toward town. Marric and Gordon Jeffers tugged at their reins and started up the road toward their destination.

'You have much experience with the Elsons, Gordon?' Marric asked. He could feel the tension swirling within himself, and he knew that Jeffers — not a man accustomed to violence — must be feeling it, too.

'Just business,' said Jeffers. 'We're the only hardware store between here and Springfield, so they buy a lot from us. Old Howard's a good feller. Ain't seen much of Chance since he left for Wyoming. He hasn't been coming into town much since he got back. Never cared for him, though, to be honest. Always a big talker, flapping his gums.'

That's exactly what Chance Elson is, thought Marric. *Problem now, though, is people are dying because of his big mouth.*

'What about those other three we were talking about — you know them?'

'Not really,' Jeffers said. 'They've come into the store every now and then, but they ain't given us any trouble. Never liked that Bill Golding, though. He's like a tiny version of Chance.'

Marric laughed. 'Very tiny.'

They rode in silence, keeping their thoughts to themselves. The river rippled to their right, and the forests were thick with fog. The air was so cold in the autumn morning that they could see their breath.

It took just over twenty minutes to reach the gate of the Bar E. Both men halted before passing through.

'You got a plan in mind, Marshal?' asked Jeffers.

Marric scratched his chin absently, squinting toward the house. 'They're likely in the bunkhouse right now — either that, or the cook shack. I should probably stop in at the main house and see if Howard's around. I'd like to have a talk with him rather than barging in and arresting his men without an explanation. If he's not around, well, we'll find the three fellers and take them into custody. They can do it the easy way or the hard way; it's up to them.'

Jeffers pushed the right side of his coat back, leaving his pistol exposed in the holster on his hip.

'I'm right with you,' he said.

Marric nodded and heeled his mount forward, Jeffers following closely behind. They passed through the gate of the Bar E and headed for the house.

8

Doyle Hunter was standing in the yard in front of the barn, smoking a cigarette. He did a double-take when he saw Marric and Jeffers approaching. Instantly, his palms began to sweat and his heart pounded.

He had met up with Golding, Clement, and Campbell the night before, when they rode into the Bar E under cover of darkness. Each man had his fair share of cuts and bruises. Golding's face had been mostly covered by a bandage. Hunter had assumed their injuries came from a fight with Jack Marric, and when he learned they had chosen to attack Burt Kroll instead, his fury was unalloyed.

'Why the hell did you go for the marshal?' he asked, trying to keep his voice down as he spoke to the three men in a small thicket of trees behind the stable. His anger was directed as much at himself for having trusted a person like Bill Golding as it was at Golding and the others.

'We couldn't get Marric,' Golding said defensively, more than a little taken aback by Hunter's words. 'He had his sister with him and he took her home in the buggy. We were waiting up the street in an alley for him, but we couldn't do anything when we saw he had the lady with him.'

'What's that got to do with Burt Kroll?'

Golding hooked his thumbs in his belt, trying not to wither under Hunter's disapproval.

'He took Marric's side at the dance. He needed to be taught a lesson.'

'Did he need to die?' Hunter was apoplectic. 'Do you realize what you've done?'

Golding looked to Clement and Campbell for support, but they avoided his gaze. 'Hell, Doyle — it got a little out of hand with the marshal. By the time we were done, we had to kill him.'

His jaw clenched, nostrils flaring, Hunter stabbed his eyes from Golding to the others and then back at the little man. He wished that Howard Elson hadn't gone out of town. The old man would have been able to handle these things much better than he had. Howard would have tamed Chance with a single word.

Damn you, Chance! Hunter thought. *This is all because of you.*

'Were you drunk?' he asked.

'I don't know if we were, uh, drunk,' Clement said. 'We'd had a few drinks, though.'

'Jesus H Christ.' Hunter shook his head in disgust. 'Did anyone see you coming or going?'

'No,' said Golding emphatically. 'I guarantee that.'

'Who put that bandage on your face?'

'Doctor Jenkins.'

'You went to his place?'

Golding seemed reluctant to respond, knowing it would only further inflame

Hunter. 'We had to,' he muttered. 'I was bleeding all over the place.'

'Did he ask who cut you?'

'Yeah, but we told him to shut up and mind his own business. He didn't ask again.'

Hunter thought things over for several seconds before saying any more. 'All right, then. What's done is done. If no one actually saw you at Kroll's place, then you might avoid a necktie party. But y'all were mighty stupid doing what you did. Mighty stupid.'

'Doyle, we — '

'Goddamn it, Bill — just shut the hell up. You three go to the bunkhouse and get some sleep. We'll see how things work out over the next few days.'

★ ★ ★

As Jack Marric and Gordon Jeffers pulled leather in front of him, Hunter knew that the moment of reckoning had arrived much sooner than he had hoped. A ray of sunlight reflected off the star on Marric's chest and Hunter was momentarily transfixed by it.

'I'm looking for Bill Golding, Hal Clement, and Jack Campbell,' Marric said plainly.

'What do you want with them?' Hunter asked.

'They murdered Burt Kroll last night,' said Marric. 'I'm taking them in and holding them until trial.'

'What makes you think you have the right to do that?'

Marric tapped the star. 'This gives me the right. I'm the marshal of Jasper now.'

'You're kidding.'

Marric turned to Jeffers. 'He thinks we're kidding.'

'We ain't kidding,' Jeffers said, looking directly at Hunter. 'Matter of fact, I've never been more serious in my life.'

Hunter shifted awkwardly on his feet. 'Who appointed you marshal?'

'The mayor and the town council,' Marric said, his patience running low.

'Now quit wasting my damn time and tell me where I can find those fellers.'

Hunter wet his lips with his tongue. The situation had gone completely out of his hands. The best he could hope to do now was to minimize the damage to himself and the Bar E.

'They're in the bunkhouse,' he rasped.

Marric and Jeffers alighted and tied their reins to the hitching post. Guns drawn, they moved across the yard toward the bunkhouse. Several Bar E hands had already emerged from the cook shack to watch the proceedings. They observed in silence, aware that something dangerous and potentially deadly was about to take place.

The bunkhouse door was ajar as the marshal and his deputy approached it. Marric stopped by the door and glanced at Jeffers, who nodded to signal his readiness. Marric pushed the door open and walked in with Jeffers close behind.

Dust swirled in the early morning

sunlight that streamed through the dirty windows. There were rows of bunks on each side of the big room. About halfway back, Golding was sleeping on a bottom bunk, snoring softly and still dressed in the clothes he had been wearing the night before. There was a bandage that ran from the corner of one eye, across his nose, down to his jaw. Blood had soaked through it. On the bunk above him was Hal Clement, also sleeping, although he had stripped down to his long johns. On the top bunk directly across the aisle from Clement was Jack Campbell, sleeping soundly on his right side, facing toward the back of the bunkhouse.

Marric and Jeffers walked down the aisle. While Jeffers covered Campbell, Marric approached Bill Golding, whose stockinged feet protruded from beneath his blanket. After a brief internal debate about the course of action, Marric decided on a direct approach. He raised his heavy Navy Colt and smashed it down on

Golding's ankle. The man screamed in pain and immediately sat upright, his greasy hair sticking out in all different directions. His face reflected pure shock when he recognized the man who had awakened him.

'Marric!' he sputtered, rubbing his ankle. 'What the hell do you think you're doing?'

'Shut your damn mouth,' Marric said. 'Get up. You're under arrest.'

'Under arrest? For what?'

'You know damn well what for, you sorry sack of shit.'

'Hell, you're loco. I ain't done nothing.'

'You killed Burt Kroll,' Marric said. 'That's a hanging offense.'

Golding snorted. 'Who says I killed Burt Kroll?'

'I do. Now get up!' Marric slammed the pistol into Golding's shin, and again the cowboy cried out.

'Who the hell are you to try to arrest me?'

'I'm the marshal now.'

'You're kidding!'

Marric reached across and grabbed the front of Golding's shirt, yanking the man to his feet. He shoved him out into the aisle.

'What the hell happened to your face?' he asked.

'None of your damn business!'

Marric glanced at Jeffers. 'Looks like Burt dished out some punishment.'

When he turned back, he noticed Clement was now awake. He had sat up and was watching attentively.

Marric pointed at him. 'You — get your ass off that bunk and get down here. We're taking you in, too.'

Clement jumped down on to the floor, his feet sending dust into the air when he landed. He glared at the marshal, but obeyed the order, walking around to stand beside Golding.

Gordon Jeffers had been distracted by the exchange between Marric and the others. He turned his head back toward the bunk where Campbell was lying just as the man rolled over to face him. From beneath the blankets, Campbell's right hand emerged. Jeffers didn't have time to give a warning before a muzzle flashed and the sound of a gunshot reverberated throughout the bunkhouse. The bullet passed through Jeffers' left ear and then Campbell was out of the bed, having leapt into the narrow walkway between the bunks and the south wall of the bunkhouse. He was crouched, using the bunks for cover, as he ran toward the back door of the building.

'You cover them!' Marric commanded, and Jeffers turned his pistol on Golding and Clement as Marric ran down the centre aisle in pursuit. The deputy's head was bleeding badly and there was a persistent ringing in his ears, but apart from that he was unscathed.

Campbell had reached the last row of bunks when he pivoted and fired off a shot at Marric. Marric dived to the floor, and the bullet entered a wooden beam on a nearby bed, sending splinters down on his head. He looked up and Campbell fired again, clearly afraid of being exposed in the ten-foot gap of open space between the last bunk and the door that led out back. The bullet came closer to Marric this time, but still it missed, shattering a window instead.

Marric looked under the bunks toward Campbell's position just as the desperate man made his break for the door. Marric could see his feet and the lower part of his legs moving rapidly across the plank floor. He swiftly took aim and fired, not sure whether he would connect. His aim was true, however, and the bullet took Campbell directly through his left Achilles tendon, shattering the bone and emerging from the front of his leg. Campbell howled and went down like a poled steer, the pistol flying from his grasp and skittering across the floor toward the far wall.

Marric lunged to his feet and approached the fallen man. Campbell sobbed, clutching his bleeding ankle.

'You bastard!' he grated. 'I'll kill you for this!'

Marric raised his boot and kicked Campbell hard in the face, causing the man's head to snap sideways. His body sagged on the floor, his eyes rolled back in his head. He was alive, but it would be a while before he regained consciousness.

Marric grabbed one of Campbell's arms and dragged the limp form up the aisle to where Jeffers stood covering Golding and Clement. He dropped Campbell at their feet and looked at the two prisoners standing before him.

'If either of you want to get cute like he did, go ahead,' he said. 'I won't be so kindly next time. Now you two pick him up and bring him outside.'

Golding and Clement seemed stunned, but they knelt and lifted Campbell by his arms. Marric waved his gun toward the door and they dragged Campbell through it. They let him fall in the grass outside.

All of the Bar E hands who weren't at work in the fields had exited the cook shack and gathered in the yard. They watched from a distance, saying nothing.

Jack Marric pulled a long handkerchief from his coat pocket and knelt beside Campbell. He tied it firmly around his injured leg, a few inches above the gunshot wound.

'That should help until we get the sawbones to look him over,' he said.

Doyle Hunter approached them, an anxious expression on his face.

'We'll bail y'all out as quick as we can,' he said to Golding. 'Of course, it will come out of your wages.'

'Out of our wages?' Golding yelled, wincing from the pain of his facial injury. 'Hell, you were the one who — '

Hunter's brows drew together. 'Shut your mouth, Bill,' he snapped. 'You better be real careful about what you say.'

'What's that supposed to mean?' Marric asked.

'Nothing,' Hunter said, never taking his eyes off Golding's face. 'It don't mean nothing.'

'Fine, then,' Marric replied, but with suspicion in his voice. 'Have some of your boys fetch these fellers' horses for the ride back to town.'

Hunter turned and called out an order. Within two minutes, three of the Bar E hands had emerged from the stable with the prisoners' horses. Campbell was now conscious. Jeffers removed some lengths of rope from his saddle-bag and tied the men's wrists behind their backs. Marric and Jeffers then helped them into their saddles. They led the three horses over to the hitching post where their own mounts were tied.

As they climbed on to their horses, the screen door of the main house opened and Chance Elson emerged. His face had been stitched up, but it was still swollen and discolored. He limped slightly as he made his way down the steps.

'What the hell is going on here?' he called.

Marric hipped in the saddle. 'Hello, Chance. Good to see you're up and about.'

'Answer my damn question!'

'We've arrested these fellers for the murder of Burt Kroll,' said Marric calmly. 'They're going to jail until trial. I don't think the judge will set bail for them.'

'Burt Kroll? He's dead?'

Elson's surprise seemed genuine, as far as Marric could tell. He wondered if Golding, Clement, and Campbell had acted without Elson's knowledge. He intended to ask them some hard questions when they got back to Jasper.

'Yeah, he's dead. Someone killed him after the dance last night.' Marric pointed at the bound men. 'These three tried to start something there, but Burt shut them down. Looks like they didn't take kindly to that.'

'You got no proof!' Golding said. Part

of his bandage was now hanging off his face.

Marric shrugged. 'Tell it to the judge.'

Elson pointed at the star on Marric's chest. 'You're the marshal now?' he asked incredulously.

'That's right. Appointed by the mayor himself, along with the town council.'

Mouth agape, Elson looked at Jeffers and then back at Marric. He seemed to have lost the power of speech.

Marric said, 'All right, Gordon. Let's head out.'

'You heard him!' Jeffers said to the three men who sat their horses with hands tied behind their backs. Golding, Clement, and Campbell kneed their horses toward the gate, with Marric and Jeffers bringing up the rear.

9

Chance Elson was drunk. It was ten o'clock at night, and he had been drinking for more than twelve hours. The whiskey helped ease his headache, and it bolstered his confidence, which had collapsed after Jack Marric had beaten him senseless in front of his own men.

After the doctor had stitched him up, he had spent the rest of the day in bed, sinking further and further into despondency. He had been cut down to size, and brutally so. He had been browbeating and dominating the crew of the Bar E ever since he returned from Wyoming. It was how he had always interacted with the people who worked for him and his father. It made him feel powerful and superior, and no one had ever had the courage to challenge him.

No one except for Jack Marric.

He thought of his father. On the one hand, he was relieved that Howard Elson had been out of town when Marric came to the Bar E. If the old man had seen the humiliation that his son had suffered at Marric's hands, he would have been deeply ashamed — maybe even sent him away again, like he had before.

On the other hand, Howard Elson might have been able to defuse the situation before things got out of hand. He had always liked Jack, and there had been a mutual respect between them that Chance had never felt he shared with his father. This was one of the main reasons for the dislike he had felt for Marric ever since they were children.

Now, with the arrest of three of the Bar E men for the murder of Burt Kroll, things had taken a decisive turn for the worst. Chance's father wasn't due home for a few days yet, but one could only imagine what his reaction would be when he heard the news.

There was no question about one thing, however: Howard Elson would blame his son for everything that had occurred in his absence.

His thoughts turned to Holly Shay, the woman he had hoped to marry. She had abandoned him for Marric, and he had no doubt that she would have married Jack if her father hadn't intervened and stopped the relationship from proceeding. Chance had hoped she would see the error of her ways and come back to him, but she had continued to shun him. Eventually she married a rich lawyer from Salem and moved away. His descent into drunkenness and violence had started with her rejection. In many ways, his life had never recovered from it.

Chance Elson drained the rest of the whiskey from his glass and slammed it down on the bedside table. He swung his legs off the side of the bed and sat upright, cursing the way his head was swimming. His fingers felt gingerly around the stitches on his lips, and he ran his tongue across the parts of his gums where there had once been teeth. The physical wounds were almost as grievous as the mental wounds. *Almost.*

His head finally cleared and he pushed himself to his feet. He carried his tumbler with him to the table across the room. He paused to splash more whiskey into the glass, and then he went out into the foyer. Through the large window by the front door, he looked out at the misty pastures that surrounded the cluster of Bar E buildings. He could see the dim shapes of the cattle through the mist, and the dark form of the big wrought-iron gate.

I need some fresh air, he thought.

He carried his whiskey with him as he opened the front door and stepped out on to the porch. To his right was the big rocking chair where his mother had often passed her days, knitting or reading. He sat down in the chair and pulled a cigar from his pocket. He toasted it carefully, then pushed it between his lips and lighted it. He released a thick plume of cigar smoke that lingered in the air before him before the wind carried it away. Then he saw a horseman pass through the gates and begin to make his way toward the house.

For a moment, Chance Elson thought he was seeing things. Then a pang of fear ran through him. Was it Jack Marric, coming back to arrest him? He shook his head. He hadn't broken any laws, after all. But Marric was an unpredictable man, and dangerous to boot.

Elson rose and hurried into the house. He fetched his pistol from the bedroom and went back out on to the porch to watch the approach of the strange rider. He seated himself again in the rocking chair, placing the pistol on the chair beside his leg. He continued to puff the cigar as he watched the rider come closer to the porch.

The man entered the yard and rode past the barn and the cook shack. To his left, the bunkhouse was in darkness. Elson knew the stranger must have seen the burning ember at the tip of his cigar. The man pulled leather and dismounted. Holding the reins, he walked his horse up to the steps in front of the house.

'Chance Elson,' he said, in a voice that Elson found familiar but which he couldn't place off the top of his head.

'That's my name,' he replied, and his right hand slipped down to grip the butt of his pistol.

'I'll be damned — you don't recognize me, do you?' The man's tone was faintly taunting.

'Should I recognize you?' Elson asked, plainly irritated.

'I'm your cousin!'

'Huh?' Elson said, leaning forward.

The man laughed. 'It's Chet, you old fool!'

Through the haze of whiskey that clouded his brain, Chance Elson had a revelation. Chet — his cousin. Chet Harper!

'Chet!' he called. He stood up and walked to the edge of the porch. 'I haven't seen you in — hell, I don't even know how long.'

Harper grinned and climbed the steps. The men embraced and clapped each other on the back.

'It's been seven or eight years,' Harper said. 'The last time I was here was that summer when I worked for your pa.'

'I remember that!'

'We had some good times then, didn't we?'

'You bet we did,' Elson agreed. He was so happy to see his cousin that he nearly forgot about Jack Marric. 'It's damn good to see you.' He jerked a thumb toward the door. 'Come on in and have some whiskey.'

'Don't mind if I do.'

They passed through the foyer and entered Elson's bedroom. He found another glass and poured for Harper, who sat down in a chair before sipping the liquor.

'Damn, that's nice,' he said. In the lantern light, he could see Elson's face much more clearly than he had out on the porch. 'Lord, Chance! What the hell happened to you?'

Elson grimaced. 'It's a long story.'

'Well, I got time.'

'I'll tell you about it later. What about you? What're you doing in Jasper?'

Harper rolled some whiskey around in his mouth before answering. 'I'm looking for someone,' he said.

'In Jasper?'

'Yeah.'

'Who are you looking for?'

Harper's kept his eyes fixed on his drink. 'The bastard who killed my brothers.'

'Killed your brothers?' Elson exclaimed, choking on his whiskey. Harper nodded slowly, saying nothing. 'When did your brothers get killed?'

'Four days ago.'

'In Roseburg?'

'Yep.'

'Where were you?'

'I was in Klamath Falls, at my sister's. Matt and Gil were supposed to come out there in a day or two. Evidently they got drunk and got into some argument with some feller at the saloon. Next thing you know, he shoots them both dead.'

'Matt and Gil wouldn't go down without a fight,' Elson observed.

'Way I heard it, he didn't even give them a chance to draw,' Harper explained, although he knew it wasn't the truth. 'They'd have killed him if he hadn't been a bushwhacking coward.'

Elson rose and refilled his and Harper's glasses.

'How did you know he's in Jasper?'

'I got some information from one of the fellers at the saloon. He saw the whole thing go down.' Harper looked again at Elson's mangled face. The crooked nose cast an elongated shadow. 'You look like you got kicked by a mule, Chance.'

'I'd have preferred that,' Elson said sourly.

'Where's your pa?'

'He's in Medford. Been there a week. He'll be back in three days.'

'He ain't going to be pleased when he sees what happened to you.'

'I know that.'

'Who did it?'

'Feller from town. Used to work for Pa. He came out here looking for work and got lippy with me. He sucker punched me and kicked the hell out of me when I was down.'

Bitterness was etched across Elson's face. He tossed the empty tumbler in the air a few times, catching it, and then his face twisted with anger and he threw the glass at the dresser. It exploded, spraying shards of glass across the expensive rug.

'Goddamn Jack Marric!' he snarled.

Chet Harper looked at him sharply. 'What did you just say?'

Elson was startled by Harper's reaction. 'I said, 'Goddamn Jack Marric.''

'Jack Marric?'

'Yeah — that's his name. The feller who did this to me.'

'I'll be goddamned,' Harper muttered.

'Why? You know him?'

'He's the son of a bitch who killed my brothers.'

Elson's scalp tightened. 'Who told you that?'

'Like I said, I had a friend in the saloon who saw him kill Gil and Matt. He recognized Marric. That's all I had when I came here — the name Marric, and that he was from Jasper.'

'You're not kidding around with me, are you?' Elson asked, suddenly suspicious.

'I don't find this funny at all,' Harper said coldly. 'I wouldn't joke about this. By God, I'm telling you the damn truth!'

A tingle snaked down Chance Elson's spine, and he knew that he had made a mistake by asking that question. Although he hadn't seen his cousin in years, he knew that Chet

Harper was a dangerous man, a man who had killed more than once in his life. He had no doubt that Chet had done things that would horrify him. He felt compelled to placate Harper.

'Aw, I know you weren't kidding, Chet,' he said, his voice a little strained.

Harper carefully set his tumbler on the small table next to his chair. He raised his head and met Elson's gaze.

'Where can I find this ... Jack Marric?'

10

Mayor Smith saw the five men ride into town. He emerged from the café and stood on the plank sidewalk as they passed him. He nodded at Marric. He had known the man could do the job, and he had been vindicated in that belief. He watched as they halted before the combined marshal's office and jail. Marric and Jeffers helped Golding and the others down. Smith wondered where Golding had acquired the wounds to his face. After a few minutes, he made his way down the street and tapped on the door to the marshal's office.

Gordon Jeffers pulled the door open and grinned. 'Come on in, Elmer,' he said. 'We just finished locking them up.'

Smith entered the office just as Jack Marric came in through the door to the cell block. The mayor caught a brief glimpse of the men in the cells before Marric closed the door. Smith smiled and patted his shoulder.

'Well done, Marshal,' he said.

'It don't bring back Burt Kroll,' Marric replied. He sat down on the corner of the desk. 'I guess it's a step in the right direction, though.'

Smith's exuberance evaporated. 'Yes, Burt. It's a damn shame. I hope your sister's holding up.'

'Me, too.' Marric rubbed his eyes with his fingertips. 'You said something about finding someone else to take over this job. How you going to go about that?'

'I'll get in touch with the sheriff and explain the situation to him. If I put some pressure on him, he'll probably be able to send a deputy out here on a short-term basis, at least until we find someone permanent.'

'It will probably take a few days to arrange for a deputy, won't it?' Marric asked.

Smith nodded. 'Yeah, I reckon it will.'

'Well, I'll just have to do my best until then. I suppose I should make my rounds.'

'Everybody in town has heard about Burt. They know you're the marshal now.'

Marric rose. 'Good. That will save me some time if I don't have to do much explaining.' He glanced at Jeffers. 'Thanks for your help, Gordon. I couldn't have done it without you.'

'Glad to help,' Jeffers said. 'Those fellers are a danger to this community. By the way, Mayor — any idea how long it will take for them to go to trial?'

'I'll have to talk to the judge,' Smith said, pursing his lips thoughtfully. 'He likes to move fast.'

Jeffers put his hand on the door handle and turned it. 'If you need any help, Jack, you know where to find me.'

'Thanks, Gordon.'

Jeffers opened the door and went out to the sidewalk. Smith followed, and then Marric came out, locking the door behind him. He walked up the street, and soon he became aware that he was the centre of attention. People watched him from behind the windows of the shops and offices. He smiled and nodded, grateful that he wasn't being forced into any conversations. The residents of Jasper seemed to know that their new lawman had a lot on his mind.

Having concluded his uneventful rounds, Marric returned to the law office. He paused near the steps leading upstairs to Kroll's room, then decided to look inside. His boots reverberated on the wooden steps and he noticed blood on the landing. When he opened the door, there was considerably more blood — on the floor and the walls. He wondered how much of the blood had come from the grotesque slash to Bill Golding's face.

Some of the furniture had been overturned. It was apparent that there had been a tremendous struggle.

After a few minutes, Marric descended the steps and went into the office. He sat down at the desk and put his hat on the blotter. He realized he didn't have anything to do.

A grating voice called out from the cell block.

'Hey, Marric!' It was Bill Golding. 'You out there?'

Marric sat there for several seconds, and then he rose and pulled the keys from his pocket. He unlocked the door to the cell block and walked back into the jail, stopping before the single large cell.

'What do you want, Tiny?' he asked.

Hal Clement laughed, and Golding glared at him for a moment before turning back to Marric.

'We're hungry,' he said. 'We ain't eaten a thing since yesterday. As prisoners, we're entitled to some food.'

'That so?'

'Yeah, that's so.'

'Who told you that?'

'It's . . . it's in the Constitution!'

'That so?' asked Marric. 'Hmmm. Well, I'll make sure you get at least one meal a day. How's bread and water sound?'

'Bread and water? You trying to be funny?'

'Not at all. Y'all will be fed at sundown. See you then.'

Marric turned and went back into the office, the cell block door clanging shut behind him. Golding was still yelling, but he gave up after a couple of minutes. Marric sat back down but soon became restless. He studied the Wanted dodgers that he found in the top drawer of Kroll's desk, but found little of interest in them. He went out and made his afternoon rounds, then had a late lunch at the café. He stood on the steps in front of the law office and smoked a few cigarettes, wondering if the mayor had sent a telegram to the sheriff about sending a deputy to town to take over. He doubted it.

When it was nearly six o'clock, Marric went to the café and bought a loaf of bread, which he took back to the jail with him. He filled a pail with water from the well out back. When he entered the cell block, he found

Golding waiting for him at the bars. Clement and Campbell were dozing on the bunks at the back of the cell.

'Get up if you want to eat,' Marric called, halting a few feet from where Golding was standing.

'That's our supper?' Golding asked.

'I explained the menu to you earlier, didn't I?' Marric replied.

Clement and Campbell rose and approached the front of the cell. Marric tore the loaf into three roughly equal chunks and handed two pieces through the bars. Clement and Campbell ate them with alacrity; both were clearly ravenous.

Marric held up the third chunk of bread in front of Golding.

'Ain't you hungry, Bill?'

Golding crossed his arms. 'I ain't eating that,' he declared petulantly.

'All right, then,' Marric said. 'I guess Hal and Jack can share it.'

He began to tear the bread in half, and Golding relented.

'Hey!' he yelled. 'Give me that.'

He reached through the bars and Marric smiled as he put the bread in the man's small hand. Golding, too, was obviously famished. Marric filled a tin cup with water and passed it through, allowing each man to drink his fill. When they were finished, he turned down the wick on the lantern that hanged on the wall across from the cell.

'Y'all have a nice night,' he said.

The prisoners glared at him, saying nothing. He crossed into the office, locking the cell block door behind him. It was getting dark now, so he lighted the lantern on the desk. He decided to make his evening rounds and then perhaps have dinner at the café.

The town was characteristically quiet, and he was just unlocking the door to his office when he spotted Gordon Jeffers coming toward him on the sidewalk. Marric grinned and waved.

'Evening, Gordon,' he said.

Jeffers nodded and shook Marric's hand. 'Evening,' he said. 'I was thinking — would you like me to serve as jailer tonight? You could go home and get some rest. I'm sure Marijo would like to see you. You could relieve me in the morning.'

Marric considered the offer for a moment, then nodded gratefully.

'That's very kind of you, Gordon,' he said. 'I think I'll take you up on that.'

He took Jeffers into the office and gave him the keys. There was a cot in the office near the wood-stove, and they found a blanket in a cabinet. Jeffers had his pistol and Marric had full confidence in his ability to handle the prisoners, all three of whom were now sleeping soundly.

At seven-thirty, Marric left the office and retrieved his horse from the livery. He rode out, his mind occupied by worried thoughts about his sister.

* * *

Marijo Marric had been in bed almost the entire day, ever since she received word of Kroll's murder. She

152

had alternated between fitful dozing and prolonged spells of crying. Her mother had tended to her, with help from Floyd Marric. They hadn't attempted to tell her everything would be fine, or that she needed to calm down, or that it was all part of God's plan. They had simply tried to make her as comfortable as they could, and they let her know they loved her.

Sarah and Floyd were in nearly as much shock as their daughter was. They had loved Kroll almost like a son, and they appreciated how happy Marijo was to be marrying him. Now that happiness had been cruelly taken away from her; they both knew her life would never be the same again.

Marijo had eaten some soup during the early afternoon, but she declined to eat dinner. It was getting dark when Floyd went out the back door to get some firewood. He walked over to the side of the house where they kept the wood in a lean-to. Jack had chopped up a lot more wood the day before, almost completely replenishing the family's supply.

Floyd's arms were full of firewood as he approached the back porch. He put a foot on the bottom step and then froze in place when a piercing shriek came from inside the house. He recognized the agonized voice as that of his daughter.

'Marijo!' he cried, dropping the wood as he scrambled up the steps and went into the kitchen. He saw his wife lying on her back on the living room floor, her white hair streaked with blood. Momentarily disoriented, he ran toward her and knelt beside her still body. Her eyes were open, staring vacantly at the roof. He knew immediately that she was dead.

'Good God!' he muttered, and then he remembered Marijo. He looked toward the hallway that led to the cabin's two bedrooms. Marijo's door was open. Beyond her room was his own, and it was there that he kept his pistol and rifle.

He cat-footed to the fireplace and grasped a solid iron poker. He could see a large shadow moving in the light that spilled out of Marijo's bedroom. He moved slowly toward the doorway, holding the poker in both hands, ready to strike.

'Whoever you are,' he called, 'come on out of there. I have a gun.' Marijo's terrified whimpers carried out into the hallway. There was no other reply to Floyd's words. 'Damn it, come out of there!'

Marric moved down the hall and halted just outside his daughter's door.

A voice thundered out to him — a man's voice, cruel and confident.

'Shut up, you old fool!' it ordered. 'Come on where I can see you. If you don't, the lady dies.'

Marric knew he had no choice but to comply. He dropped the poker and stepped into the doorway. He cried out when he saw the scene inside.

A large man in dirty range clothes stood beside his daughter's bed. His left hand gripped Marijo's hair, twisting her neck painfully. His right hand held a pistol, the muzzle pressed against the woman's temple.

'Who — who are you?' Floyd asked, his voice not quite steady.

'You'll find out all you need to know about me soon enough,' said the man with the gun. 'Where's your son?'

The old man was confused. 'My son?'

'Yeah — Jack. Your goddamn son!'

'He's in town, at the jail.'

'I guess I'm going to have to find a way to get his attention,' said the intruder. He took the gun away from Marijo's head and pointed it at Floyd Marric. Marric stared back at him, enveloped in dread.

Then the man fired and Floyd went down.

11

When he saw the fire, Jack Marric had just reached the trail that branched off the main road out of Jasper and led to his family home. The trees were thinner here, and he could discern the flames licking upward into the night sky.

Marric dug his spurs into his horse's flanks and the animal burst forward, racing up the trail toward the blazing cabin. When they reached the edge of the trees, the horse began to panic, leaping upward on its hind legs, its eyes rolling with fear. Marric leapt from the saddle and ran toward the house, instinctively drawing his pistol as he did so.

The entire place was aflame. If any people were inside it, they were surely dead.

Still, Marric had to look for himself. He ran around the side of the house toward the back. The smoke was heavy, the wind carrying it across his path. Suddenly his foot caught on something in the grass and he tumbled forward to the ground. He heard a grunt as he went down, followed by labored wheezing. On his hands and knees, he crawled back a few feet, and there he found his father.

Floyd Marric was near death. He had been shot in the left shoulder, and his face and clothes were smudged with black soot from the fire. Smoke rose in thin wisps from his shirt and hair. But somehow, miraculously, he still lived.

Marric dropped to his knees and put his hands on his father's face. He cradled his head in his lap.

'Pa!' he hollered. 'Pa! Can you hear me?'

Floyd coughed some more, blinking uncertainly. 'Jack?' he said.

'Yes, Pa. It's me. Where are Ma and Marijo?'

'Ma is . . . dead,' Floyd said, and he emitted a tormented groan. 'Lord have mercy, Jack. Your ma is dead.'

Tears streamed out of Floyd's eyes and trickled down his grimy cheeks.

'What happened, Pa?' Marric asked, his own eyes pooling with tears. At that moment, he suddenly remembered Marijo. 'Where's Marijo?'

'A . . . a man took her . . . '

'*What?*'

'He took her.' Floyd's chest heaved as he tried to take a breath. He had inhaled so much smoke that the process was difficult. 'Killed your . . . ma. Took Marijo.'

'What man?' pleaded Marric, his mind reeling. 'Who did this?'

'He . . . didn't give a name.'

'Did you recognize him?'

Floyd shook his head, the movement barely perceptible.

'Was he one of Elson's men?'

'I don't . . . think so,' Floyd said, his voice fading.

'Did he say anything, Pa? Anything at all?'

Floyd Marric was still, and for a

desperate moment it appeared that he was dead. Then his lips moved once more.

'He said he was taking her to the . . . old mill in Lowell,' he murmured. Marric had to place his ear very close to his father's lips to make out his words. 'He said . . . he wanted you.'

'Me? He wants me?'

Floyd nodded faintly. 'He said for you . . . to come alone. Tomorrow at . . . midnight. If you come sooner . . . he'll . . . kill . . . '

The words died off and a soft rattling sound came from the old man's throat. Marric knew his father was gone. He continued to kneel there in the grass, holding him. There was a numbness within him that he had never felt before, as if he had left his body and was observing the scene from a distance.

He stayed in that same position for well over an hour, until the fire began to burn itself out. Then a cold rain began to fall, the drops sizzling among the flames that remained. The rain seemed to return Marric to his senses, at least a little. It fell on him for twenty minutes, and then he rose, lifting his father's body.

He carried it behind the charred ruin of the cabin toward the stable. He laid the body in the grass for a moment while he opened the stable door, then he carried it in and placed it atop a large pile of hay. He lighted a lantern and turned it up to its full brightness.

Lantern in hand, Marric went out of the stable and approached the smoldering remains of the family home. He stopped in his tracks about five feet from where the back door had been. There in the grass at his feet was an empty jug of coal oil. Now he knew what had been used to start the fire, and why the fire had burned so powerfully. He kicked the empty jug and it rolled away, disappearing into some bushes near the edge of the yard.

He went toward the house and stepped through a massive hole where the kitchen wall had once been. A few posts remained standing, although they were blackened and stunted. Only the stone chimney had survived the fire largely unscathed.

He explored for half an hour, moving piles of ash and debris, but he found no trace of his mother's remains. She had been so small and fragile, and the fire had been so intense. There was nothing left of her now.

He returned to the stable and closed the door. The only sound was that of the rain, hammering against the walls. There were two blankets folded on a shelf in the corner, and he removed them both. He covered his father's body with one of them, and then he lay down beside him and spread the other blanket over himself. Within a few minutes he had fallen into a merciful slumber.

★　★　★

Dawn had just begun to spread its varied hues across the heavens when Jack Marric awoke. He lay there for a long moment, aware of deep despair within himself, his mind not quite able to grasp its origins. And then it all came back to him, every detail: the fire, his mother's death, his father's words and last, futile gasps for life.

And Marijo. The killer who destroyed Marric's family had taken Marijo.

He was to face this man at midnight, at the abandoned mill out in Lowell.

He wondered at the location. Only someone who was familiar with the area would choose it. He thought of his sister, a prisoner there. For all he knew, she was already dead. He would put nothing past the killer. Whoever had taken her had used her to lure Marric — that much was clear. He was the real target, and his family had paid the ultimate price for that.

Who was this man? How did he know Jack Marric? What had Marric done to spark such lethal hatred in him?

His mind went over these thoughts time and again, and then he banished them. The answers would come soon enough, he knew. They would come at midnight.

After that, Marric could live or die; he cared little either way now. But one thing was certain — he would kill the man who had done this to his family.

12

Jack Marric buried his father at the south end of the yard, just where the grass met the trees. There was a large apple tree there that Floyd had always loved, and Marric could think of no better place for his father to rest than beneath that tree. He fashioned a cross and placed it at the head of the grave. His father hadn't been a religious man by any means, but his mother had been, and Marric knew she would have been pleased by the gesture.

If only he had been able to find her, or what was left of her, and bury her beside her husband. As he gazed at the tidy mound of earth and rocks that formed his father's grave, Marric thought of his parents and of the life they had given him, right on this very land. He had never, he realized, heard an angry word pass between them.

Their marriage hadn't been perfect — particularly in earlier years,when Floyd had struggled with the demon liquor — but they had persevered and done their best, always having the best interests of their children in mind.

Self-recrimination lurked within Marric. He had brought this all down on his family — somehow, he was responsible for what had happened. He had no idea who the killer was, but the man had punished Marric's parents and sister to get back at him. He had only been home for a matter of days; he now bitterly regretted the years he had spent away, pursuing a frivolous life and neglecting his true responsibilities.

Again, he forced such thoughts from his mind. He put his hands over his eyes and breathed deeply. The rain had been reduced to a thin drizzle now. Marric removed his hat and spoke.

'Pa, I'm sorry it came to this,' he said. 'I never meant to bring no harm to you, or to Ma, or to Marijo.' He paused, a furrow creasing his brow. 'I'm going to make this right, one way or another. I'm going to make the son of a bitch pay. I promise.'

He placed his Stetson firmly back on his head. His horse had returned when he started digging the grave, and now he climbed into leather and touched spurs, urging the animal on to the road to Jasper.

★ ★ ★

As he rode up Main Street, everyone on the side-walks stopped to look at him. He could feel their eyes upon him as he made his way through the mud. He knew he looked terrible — his clothes covered in dirt, soot, and ash, his face smeared with the same. He couldn't have cared less. He didn't turn his head to acknowledge their stares. He was indifferent to anything but that which he needed to do between now and midnight.

He stopped in front of the law office

and dismounted. The door opened as he climbed the stairs and Gordon Jeffers stood there, regarding Marric with alarm. He moved aside to let the marshal into the office.

'Judas priest, Jack! What happened?' he asked.

Marric removed his hat and dropped it on the desk. When he spoke, his voice was soft.

'Someone killed my ma and pa,' he said. 'Burned down the house.'

Jeffers' mouth fell open with shock. 'But — who? Who would do that?'

'I don't know,' Marric replied, staring at a point on the wall. 'I asked my pa before he passed on. He said he didn't know the man.'

'Could it be another of Chance Elson's boys?' Jeffers ventured.

'I asked Pa that. He said he didn't recognize the feller as a Bar E man.'

Jeffers struck his forehead. 'What about Marijo?'

Marric shifted his gaze to Jeffers' face. 'The killer took her.'

'Took her? Where?' Jeffers seemed almost unable to believe what he was hearing, although he didn't doubt that every word was true. Terribly true.

'To the old mill in Lowell. Don't ask me why he chose that place, but that's what my pa told me. Evidently this feller wanted him to pass on the message.'

'Is that where you're heading now?'

Marric shook his head. 'Bastard said to be there tonight, at midnight. Said if I come any sooner, he'll kill Marijo.'

Jeffers straightened. 'I'll come with you.'

'I appreciate that, Gordon, but he said that if I bring anyone else with me, he'll kill her.'

'Maybe we can split up — I could ride around and go in from the back.'

Marric's chiseled features were grave. 'I can't take that chance,' he said. 'Not with Marijo's life. I can't do it.'

'I . . . I understand, Jack,' said Jeffers. 'Of course.'

'Did those fellers give you any

trouble last night?' Marric asked, nodding toward the cell-block door.

'No, nary a peep. Mayor came in this morning and said a deputy's going to be coming out to take them to the county jail. Sheriff told the mayor he can't spare a man to take your job just yet.'

'I ain't worried about it,' Marric said. 'I can work that out down the road. Only thing I'm thinking about right now is getting Marijo.' He tugged gently at his beard, his mind elsewhere. 'That and killing the son of a bitch.'

Jeffers saw the grim, granite-like resolution in Jack Marric. He didn't envy any man who went against Marric tonight.

'What're you going to do now?' he asked.

Marric exhaled, and some of the tension seemed to go out of him. 'I'm going to buy a second pistol,' he said. 'Then I'm going to the hotel to have a bath and sleep a little. Then I'm going to have a big supper. I want to be fresh when I get out there tonight.'

'I'll stay on here,' Jeffers said. 'Don't worry about a thing.'

Marric reached out and the men shook hands firmly.

'Thanks, Gordon,' he said. 'I won't forget it.'

He released Jeffers' hand and strode out of the office. His boots thudded on the planks outside as he made his way down the block to the general store.

*   *   *

The smell inside the half-collapsed old mill was horrible. It reeked of animal droppings and dead rodents. The building hadn't been used in twelve years, ever since a fire destroyed almost half of it. The rest had stood, unused and unmaintained, the boards rotting and warping with the passage of time, the wet winters and the hot summers.

The stranger had lashed Marijo to a rickety old wooden chair. She sat in the corner of the big room, at the end of a row of massive saws. A handkerchief was tied tightly around her head, covering her mouth, into which another handkerchief had been stuffed. She had to breathe through her nose or she would suffocate. At first it had induced a panicky feeling in her, but she forced herself to calm down.

Through a shattered window just a few feet away, Marijo could see the man standing on a large rock, urinating down the hill. His back was to her and she shivered as she looked at him. She didn't know what to make of this malevolent force that had entered her room the night before. He almost didn't seem human — he was more like some strange beast, like something evil from a fairy tale. But he was real, and what she had witnessed last night was certainly not a dream.

Her mother and father were dead. Although the latter had been clinging to life when the stranger took her away, Marijo had known that he wasn't long for this world. She had heard every word the killer had said to Floyd Marric. She knew that he really wanted Jack, although he had obviously been enjoying himself as he killed her parents and burned down their home.

He hadn't spoken a single word to her since he thrust her on to her horse and tied her hands to the saddlehorn. She desperately wanted information, some insight into why he was doing these terrible things. She hadn't dared to ask, however. Besides, it was a bit of a relief not to have to make conversation with him.

She watched as he buttoned his pants and turned to walk back to the mill. She closed her eyes and pretended to be sleeping. He came in through a charred doorway that had long since lost its door. His footsteps approached her, and she sensed his shadow fall across her. She could hear his breathing as he stood before her, and finally she opened her eyes.

'Awake, huh?' he said. 'I knew it.'

He sat down on a bench near one of

the saw blades. He stared at her with an unnerving intensity. He removed the makings from a coat pocket and built a cigarette. Once he had lighted it, he regarded her through the smoke that trickled out of his nostrils and drifted up into the air.

'You're probably wondering who I am and why I'm here,' he observed. 'Can't say I blame you.'

Her mouth gagged, Marijo could only stare back at the man. He was large, with the rough hands and broken fingernails of a laborer. He had several days' worth of stubble on his jaw, and his teeth were dark brown and jagged. He exuded confidence — as if everything would inexorably go his way, and the outcome of his encounter with Jack at midnight were preordained.

The evil he exuded was an almost palpable thing. He seemed no more agitated over the previous night's events than if he had stepped on a few bugs. Marijo knew this wasn't his first time killing people, not by any stretch of the

174

imagination. This man was a killer, and one who took pleasure in his work. She wondered idly how many other innocent people had lost their lives at his hands.

He spoke again: 'You heard everything I told your pa, so you know your brother's coming here tonight. It'll all be over then.' He yawned. 'He'll be dead, and then I'll kill you. Then I can be on my way.'

Marijo's face was expressionless as she regarded the stranger, and he grinned at her.

'My name's Chet Harper, by the way. Your brother killed both of my brothers down in Roseburg, one week ago tomorrow. If I had been there, he'd be dead already. Lucky for him, though, I was out of town. He didn't know it, but when he killed Matt and Gil, he signed his own death warrant. Tonight I'm going to get my pound of flesh.' His features hardened, assuming an animalistic aspect. 'Nobody kills a Harper and lives. That's all there is to it.'

She watched as he rose from the bench and stretched.

'Yep, I got a real nice surprise for old Jack Marric tonight. He ain't going to know what hit him. I'm going to make it worth my while, you can be sure of that.'

13

There were ten or twelve people in the general store when Jack Marric walked in. They moved wordlessly out of his way as he walked toward the counter. There, under glass, was a display of pistols for sale. The prices, brands, and sizes varied, but Marric already knew what he wanted.

The owner of the store was named Leo. No one ever used his last name. He was bent with age, but his brown eyes sparkled behind his wire-rimmed spectacles. He came out from the back room and approached the counter.

'What can I do for you, son?' he asked.

Marric pointed at one of the pistols in the display. 'I want to buy that Navy Colt,' he said. 'And a box of bullets to go with it.'

'Yes, yes,' Leo said eagerly. 'It's

probably the best gun of the lot.'

He reached under the glass and brought out the pistol, which he handed across the counter to Marric. The marshal weighed it in his hand, opened the cylinder and spun it, looked through the barrel, and checked the hammer mechanism. Satisfied, he removed a wad of bills from his pocket as Leo placed a box of bullets in front of him. He peeled four bills from the roll and put them in the old man's palm.

'You can keep the change,' he said.

'You sure?' Leo asked.

Marric nodded curtly. 'I'm sure.'

He exited the store and crossed the street to the hotel. After he had reserved a room there, he put his horse at the livery, where he had it fed and watered. He returned to the hotel with his saddle-bags and rifle, and arranged for a hot bath in his room. He stripped naked and sat down in the bath, the hot water like a soothing balm on his flesh. He soaked for a while, then used the brush to scrub away the soot and dirt from his skin and hair. By the time he emerged from the bath, the water was nearly black.

Marric dried himself and removed his shaving supplies from one of his saddle-bags. Using the small mirror on the wall he shaved off his beard, using rapid, deft strokes of his straight razor, rendering his face smooth without leaving a nick. He brushed his hair carefully and dressed in a clean shirt and Levi's from his other saddle-bag. Then he sat down at the table and meticulously cleaned, oiled, and loaded his weapons. He drew his boot knife and tested the edge against the pad of his thumb. It was, as always, extremely sharp.

His ritual complete, Jack Marric lay down on the sagging bed and fell asleep. Just before closing his eyes, he opened his pocket watch and checked the time. The spidery hands said it was two o'clock.

When Marric opened his eyes, it was dark out. The lantern on the dresser across the room was the only illumination.

Marric sat up and looked again at his watch. Nine o'clock.

He rose and put on his boots and gunbelt. He pulled his Stetson down and descended to the lobby of the hotel. The clerk behind the desk was dozing as he passed by and went out to the street. The brisk air was invigorating. He went down a block and crossed over to the café. There were only a few customers there at this time of night, not long before closing time. Marric went to a table at the back of the room and a tired-looking middle-aged woman came in from the kitchen and greeted him warmly.

'Evening, Marshal,' she said.

'Evening, ma'am,' he replied, his voice strangely detached.

She looked at him a little more

closely and noticed there was something different about him, apart from his having shaved his beard. She could tell he wasn't in the mood for idle talk.

'What can I get you?' she asked.

He ordered a large meal and some coffee. When she had served him, he ate slowly, stopping occasionally to check his watch. He finished his meal and paid her, then walked out into the night.

He returned to his hotel room and put on his sheepskin. With his saddle-bags and his rifle, he went back down to the street and walked to the livery. The stableman was still awake, and he brought Marric's horse out of the stall. Marric saddled it, slipped his rifle into the scabbard, and put the saddle-bags back on. He walked the horse to the street and climbed up.

Main Street was practically deserted as he rode slowly toward the edge of town. He saw a light on in the law office, and the door opened as he came abreast of the small building. Gordon Jeffers stood in the doorway and nodded at Marric. Marric nodded back and continued on his way.

There was nothing to be said now, only dangers to be faced.

★   ★   ★

To ride from Jasper to Lowell would normally take about ninety minutes, but Marric took his time, his mind turning over the various scenarios of what might await him out at the mill.

He knew the location well. It was at the west end of town, in a clearing surrounded by dense forest. The cleared area around the building was expansive; there was no way for Marric to approach it without being seen.

He recalled the layout of the mill, wondering where the killer would be. Would he shoot Marric as the latter crossed the yard? Would he let Marric come into the mill before he tried to kill him? It was the first option that really worried Marric. He would be vulnerable once he came out of the trees. If he were able to get to the building in one piece, then he figured he had good odds, although the advantage would still be with the man who had killed his family and abducted his sister. The man who had destroyed so much just for a chance to kill Jack Marric.

Now he was going to get his chance.

Moonlight streamed through the leafless trees and reflected off the river that flowed past on Marric's right. He passed darkened homesteads and ranches. As he passed the gate to the Bar E, he glanced across the field toward the big house. No lights shone in its windows. Despite his father's words, Marric couldn't be sure that Chance Elson wasn't involved in the attack on his family.

Wildfowl burst from a mass of firs as Marric rounded a bend, startling him. He encountered no other people on the road as he made his way to Lowell.

The miles passed in silence, and

finally Marric saw a wide trail that branched off the main road. Once it had been used frequently, as it had led to one of the busiest lumber mills in the southern Willamette Valley; then the fire had come. The trail was now heavily overgrown.

He tugged the reins and heeled his mount off the road on to the trail. It was about half a mile to the mill. Marric rode a few dozen yards before halting and removing his watch from his coat pocket. He thumb-snapped a lucifer and held it over the face of the watch. It was ten minutes to midnight. He blew out the match and put his watch away before proceeding up the trail.

When he could see the clearing up ahead, he dismounted and moved his horse into the woods. He tied it to a birch and, hidden among the trees, moved forward until he had a clear view of the mill. He knelt between two large maples and swept his eyes over the clearing and the dilapidated, shadowy structure that stood in its centre.

There were no signs of movement in or around the mill, and no lights were visible. A thick mist covered the field.

As he had remembered, there was no way to approach the mill using stealth. Coming from any direction, one would be forced to cross the field to reach the building; that meant being exposed for roughly a hundred feet.

Marric sighed heavily. There was no other option. He would have to be alert, ready for an attack.

It was almost midnight now. Marric moved back through the trees to where he had left his horse. He led it back to the trail and mounted. He unbuttoned his sheepskin for quick access to the pistol at his hip; the other pistol was tucked into his waist-band.

His heart pounding, all of his senses alert to the danger of what he was about to do, Marric rode forward to the rim of the woods. He halted there for only a few seconds, and then he urged his mount forward, moving from the shelter of the trees to the open expanse of the field. The bottom halves of his horse's legs were obscured by the mist.

Marric had only ridden a few yards into the field when a man's voice, arrogant and self-assured, rang out from somewhere in the mill.

'Stop right there, Marric!'

Marric reluctantly complied, tugging the reins and bringing his mount to a halt. His eyes moved over the façade of the dark building, trying to pin-point the location of the speaker.

'I'm here,' Marric called, trying to get the other to speak again. 'Where's my sister?'

A laugh erupted into the darkness.

'Don't get ahead of yourself, pard.'

'This is between you and me. She ain't done nothing to you. Let her go and we'll settle this like men.'

'It ain't going to be that easy, Marric. I think when I'm done killing you, I might like to have a little fun with her. What do you think?'

An icy feeling, close to despair, filled

Marric's chest. 'Only a coward hides in the dark,' he said. 'That pretty well describes you, don't it?'

Again came the laugh. 'You're going to pay for what you done. You probably thought you got away with it, scot free, didn't you?'

'Why don't you tell me what you mean?'

The voice now went up several decibels, as if the speaker were not entirely in control of his emotions.

'My brothers, you son of a bitch! You killed my brothers!'

Marric was momentarily confused, but then the realization burst into his mind. *The Harpers — Matt and Gil.* He remembered hearing about their other brother, the one who was out of town.

A cloud moved away from the moon, which spilled its light down upon the scene.

'Your brothers were yellow-bellies! They got what they deserved.'

And then it happened. A glint of

moonlight was reflected from a window on the second floor, over to Marric's left. Virtually without thinking, Marric reached for his Navy Colt and cleared leather. He thumbed back the hammer and fired a shot at the window. At the very moment he fired, he saw a muzzle flash and heard a shot come from the window. The bullet missed him, disappearing in the field. There was a shriek of pain and Marric knew he had hit the killer. He didn't take any time to follow up, however. He leapt from the saddle and ran for the edge of the building, disappearing into the shadows.

He put his back against the wall and turned his head, listening for any sounds of movement inside. He heard some loud metallic crashing, as if equipment were being knocked over. A few feet away was a window, the glass long since smashed in. Marric hurried toward it and, putting one hand on the bottom of the window frame, jumped through it, landing on his feet. He moved forward and crouched against a wall.

It took a minute for his vision to adjust to the darkness within the mill. Only a small amount of moonlight made its way inside. He rose and moved down a narrow aisle between two rows of log rollers. He made as little noise as he possibly could. The end of the aisle led to a wide passage-way, perpendicular to the log rollers. There was enough room here for two wagons to be drawn side-by-side. Marric knelt down behind the last roller, his eyes probing the darkness.

A raccoon scurried across the walkway, and Marric raised his pistol, ready to fire, before he saw the small animal.

He looked up to the wooden landing that ran around the entire interior of the mill. There were several windows that were accessible from the landing, and he knew that this was where the killer — *Chet Harper*, for the name had come back to him — had been lurking, waiting for Marric to ride into the field.

Where was Marijo? Was she here in the mill, or had Harper left her somewhere else?

From the far corner of the cavernous room, a woman's scream answered Jack Marric's questions.

14

Still crouching, Marric hurried across the wide central passageway, moving toward the corner from which he had heard the scream. He knew who had cried out — it was Marijo. She was here, and she was alive. That was all he needed to know.

He reached the wall and turned left. This end of the building was dominated by five massive saws. The blades were still in them, left behind after the fire. They were rusty from years of disuse and exposure to the rain from the large hole in the roof. Marric walked cautiously toward the saws, and then he stopped in his tracks.

There, tied by rope to a chair, was Marijo. Around her neck hung a handkerchief that appeared to have been used for a gag. Her hair was in disarray and one of her sleeves had been torn. When she saw her brother, her eyes widened.

'Jack!'

Still holding his Navy Colt, Marric moved toward her.

'Where is he?' he called.

Chet Harper emerged from behind one of the saws, his gun extended toward Marric. A large blood stain was visible on his shoulder.

'I'm here!' he said.

Marric turned just as Harper fired. The bullet took him in the left thigh, and suddenly he was on the floor, his leg throbbing. He raised his pistol and fired twice, but the shots were wild. Harper fired again, the bullet hitting the floor a few feet from Marric.

Harper ducked back behind the saw as Marric took another shot at him. The slug ricocheted off the edge of the rusty blade. Harper leaned out, raising his pistol. Marric fired, barely missing Harper's head; then, as Harper thumbed back the hammer, Marric triggered his last bullet. The muzzle blossomed, spitting acrid death.

The shot took Harper in the hand, and he squealed as the pistol twirled out of his grip and slid across the floor beneath the saws. Blood dripped from his hand.

'I'll kill you!' he bellowed, running toward Marric.

Marric pulled the trigger again, but the hammer fell on an empty chamber. He tossed the gun and reached for the other Colt in his waistband, but it snagged on his belt and then Harper was upon him, driving his knee into Marric's injured leg and pummeling him with his fists.

The blows were relentless, and Marric came close to blacking out before putting his arms up to deflect them. Harper was in a frenzy, drops of spittle flying from his mouth.

'This is for Matt and Gil!' he snarled.

Marric managed to connect an uppercut to Harper's jaw, momentarily stunning him. The reprieve was short-lived. Harper knocked another blow aside with his elbow. He reached forward and wrapped his powerful fingers around Marric's throat, squeezing with immense force.

Marric fought to get some air, but the grip was too strong. He tried to pry the fingers from his neck; then, that failing, he smashed his fists against Harper's forearms. Nothing lessened the pressure.

Harper leaned forward, his sweating face now only a few inches from Marric's. His lips were twisted in a maniacal sneer. His eyes were almost exultant, as if this moment were the culmination of his entire life.

'I wish I would've been there that night,' he said through clenched teeth. 'I'd have killed you then.' He lifted Marric up, then slammed the back of his head on to the floor. 'You hear me? You killed my brothers — there ain't no way I'd let you get away with that!'

Marric blacked out momentarily. He felt himself moving into a strange sort of consciousness. He could hear Harper's words, but their meaning wasn't registering in his mind. His attempts to stop the strangulation weren't working, and he seemed to pass into a warm, gauzy state, as if he were being led to a peaceful, eternal slumber.

A cry from Marijo penetrated his ears.

'Jack! No!' she yelled, and somehow he knew that he couldn't surrender to the hands that gripped his throat with such determination. He blinked, focusing his gaze on Harper's face.

'That's right,' Harper said. 'It's over now.' He grinned, assured of victory. 'You're dead, Marric.'

Marric recognized his chance, and then he struck. He thrust his right thumb upward and it sank into the corner of Harper's left eye, passing between the eyelids and sinking deep into the eye socket. Blood spurted down Marric's arm, and then there was a popping feeling against his thumbnail.

Harper howled and yanked his hands away from Marric's throat. His left eye was out of the socket, hanging beside his nose but still connected to his head. He covered his injured eye with his hand and attempted to punch Marric, but Marric dodged the blow and rolled forcefully on to his side, sending Harper sprawling. Marric regained his feet but his head was spinning. He tumbled back into a work table and grasped it, trying not to fall.

To Marric's surprise, Harper managed to stand up. He removed his hand from his eye, and the sight was revolting. Blood and some kind of clear liquid streamed from the socket, and the eyeball itself seemed misshapen.

'That looks like it hurts,' said Marric, his head clearing.

Harper bellowed with rage and ran toward him. Marric suddenly remembered the other pistol and reached for it. He drew it from his waistband and began to level it, but Harper was too close. He grabbed the barrel with both hands and twisted it, brutally wrenching Marric's fingers. Harper's thumb slipped into the trigger guard and he started to turn the muzzle towards Marric's abdomen.

Marric grunted. One of his fingers felt as if it were broken, but he saw now that the moment of truth was at hand. Ignoring the pain, he, too, gripped the pistol with both hands, using all his strength to push the barrel away. The men were of almost equal size and strength, but Harper had a small advantage in both areas. That was all he might need to tip the scales in his favor.

Sweat dripped off the tip of Harper's nose and splashed against Marric's hand. Marric's arms began to shake as, very gradually, Harper began to overtake him, the black hole at the end of the barrel moving closer to his stomach.

Through his peripheral vision, Marric could see Marijo, tied to the chair. She was straining forward in her seat, as far as the ropes would allow, watching them. He had come too far to die at Harper's hand, leaving his sister at the killer's mercy.

He rammed his shoulder into Harper's chest. The big man remained on his feet at first, then his boots slipped on the moldy sawdust and he fell forward to his knees. Marric's right hand released the pistol and he reached down to his boot. Pain shot through his other wrist as Harper twisted the gun.

Marric's hand lifted the knife from his boot and the blade sank smoothly into Harper's chest. Passing through ribs, the point entered his heart and then plunged entirely through it as Marric pushed the blade all the way to the hilt.

Harper's hands unclenched and fell away from the pistol. Marric let it fall to the floor. Harper's one functioning eye rolled back in his head, and his body slid off the knife and collapsed into an untidy heap.

Marric dropped the knife beside the body. He looked toward his sister; her face was drawn but her expression was one of relief.

'Jack!' she said. 'I was so scared . . . '

He took a few halting steps toward her, and then he, too, fell to the floor, out cold.

★   ★   ★

It took nearly an hour for Marijo Marric to get one of her hands free from its bindings. Harper had tied them both very tightly, and her wrist was raw and bloody. After a few minutes she was able to get her other hand free, and then she untied the knots that bound her legs to the chair.

She stood up, her limbs throbbing from being bound. She moved on bare feet across the floor and dropped beside her brother. His breathing was steady. She decided to leave him alone for the time being.

She went out into the yard. The moon was nearly full, and the stars were dazzling in their brightness. She realized, with mild disbelief, that she was alive, and that the man who had killed her parents and taken her to this god-forsaken place was now dead. The terror was over.

She put her hands over her face and sobbed quietly, remembering her parents' terrible deaths. If only Jack had been there that night; she knew he would have been able to stop the man, the one who called himself Chet Harper.

If Burt Kroll had been there, he would have done the same. In the horrific aftermath of her kidnapping, Marijo hadn't thought of Burt once. Now she remembered him, and how he had died, and a wave of sadness and loss washed over her.

The sound of an approaching horse caught her attention. She inhaled sharply and looked toward the trail. Yes — someone was coming.

Who could it be? she wondered. Was it one of Harper's friends? Perhaps someone from Lowell who had the gunshots?

She turned and ran back through the grass into the mill. She stopped near her brother and her gaze darted around the floor. Then she saw the pistol, ran to it, and picked it up, backing into the narrow walkway between two of the saws. She pulled back the hammer and waited, her breathing shallow.

The horse was coming closer, rounding the corner of the mill and moving toward the open doorway near which she had been bound. She realized this wasn't a random citizen of Lowell, come to investigate the shooting. This was someone who knew Harper, and knew exactly where to find him.

'Hey, Chet!'

The voice was that of a young man. Marijo straightened, tension and fear gripping her.

'Chet, where you at?'

She thought she recognized the voice, although she couldn't quite place it. It was someone she knew, though; there was no question about that. How did this person know Chet Harper?

The rider halted near the doorway. Marijo was completely obscured by the saw blade. She heard the man dismount and then his boots clomped on the steps. A large rectangle of moonlight on the floor before her was partly filled with the silhouette of a figure wearing a large Stetson.

'Christ!' he gasped as he looked down at the still bodies of Chet Harper and Jack Marric.

He came into the room and moved quickly toward Harper. He leaned over and rolled the dead man on to his back. There was a hole visible in the left breast of Harper's shirt, surrounded by blood. The man recoiled when he saw the bloodied pulp of Harper's eyeball hanging from his head. The stranger stood upright and removed his hat. He pushed his fingers through his hair as he stared down at the corpse.

That was when Marijo recognized him. She had been right — this was someone she knew; indeed, someone she had known for her entire life.

'Chance Elson,' she said, her voice loud and clear.

Elson started and swung to face her.

'Oh, God!' he exclaimed. He laughed awkwardly. 'Lord, it's you — Marijo. What're you doing here?'

She stepped out from between the saws, both hands still holding the Navy Colt. It looked massive in her small, thin fingers, and it was pointed directly at Chance Elson's chest.

'I was thinking of asking you the very same question, Chance,' she said coolly.

Elson's gaze moved between the two men on the floor as he tried to come up with a plausible explanation.

'Well, uh,' he stammered. 'Someone, uh, told my foreman they wanted to meet me here.'

'For what?'

'To, uh, talk, I guess.' He shrugged helplessly.

'Who wanted to meet you here?'

'They . . . didn't say.'

Her dark eyes regarded him with open skepticism.

'So you often ride out in the middle of the night to meet strangers and talk?' she asked.

Elson was sweating. 'I guess it was Chet who done it,' he said. 'Yeah, it was him. We're cousins, you know.'

'I didn't know that.'

'Yeah, we are.' He shook his head in a show of concern. 'Lord, did Chet kill Jack?' he asked.

'Why would he do that?'

'I don't know. I guess maybe he got mad when I told him about the fight that me and Jack had. He must have took it to heart, wanted to get even.'

'Did you tell him to get even?'

Marijo's prosecutorial tone unnerved Elson. 'Hell, no! I wouldn't do that. It wasn't personal. Just a little squabble between old friends.'

He laughed again, almost pleadingly this time. 'I always liked old Jack.'

She moved a step closer. 'Do you

know what Chet Harper did?'

'No, ma'am. I don't.'

'He killed my ma and pa. Burned down our house. Brought me here and nearly killed Jack.'

'Jack's alive?' Elson asked, his voice scarcely above a whisper now.

'Yes, he's alive.'

'Well, thank God for that!' Elson said, and the words had barely left his mouth before his hand blurred down to the gun strapped to his right hip. He grabbed the butt of the pistol and pulled it up.

His thumb had just touched the hammer when Marijo fired. The bullet entered his neck, and then she let off another round. It took him in the collar-bone and he spun partially around. He turned back to face her and tried to raise his weapon, but it seemed impossibly heavy.

Marijo pulled the trigger again, then again. Chance Elson dropped his gun and staggered backward. Finally his knees buckled and he crashed down on to the floor. His lifeless eyes remained open, staring upward at the pale moon through the hole in the roof.

15

Jack Marric didn't recognize the room. The wall-paper was decidedly feminine, with roses entwined with ribbons, repeated ad nauseam. The curtains were drawn and there was a reddish glow behind them. He wasn't sure whether it was the sunrise or the sunset, and he had no idea how he had come to be where he was.

The bed on which he lay was softer than any other bed he could remember. He pulled his hand out from under the quilt and felt around his head. There were bandages there, and he saw two small splints affixed to the first and second fingers of his left hand.

The door opened and a young woman leaned in. When she saw that Marric was awake, her mouth spread into a smile.

'Pa!' she called. 'He woke up!'

He heard a man's voice in the distance, then heavy footfalls approached.

'Watch out now, darling,' the voice intoned. 'I'm going to check him over.'

The girl moved aside and a fat, florid-cheeked man with white hair and handlebar mustachios came in. He was in shirtsleeves, his pants held up by red suspenders. Marric recognized him as Dr Muller, the family doctor who had been taking care of the people of Lowell for as long as he could remember.

'My boy, I can't tell you how glad I am to see you with your eyes open,' Muller said, obviously pleased.

'Where am I?' asked Marric.

'You're in the back room here at my house,' Muller explained. 'You've been here for four days now. This is the first time we've seen you awake. That bullet wound in your leg is healing very nicely.'

'I'm in Lowell?'

Muller nodded. 'Yes. Your sister came and got me. When I got out there, you were in a bad way.'

Fragments of memory returned. 'How is Marijo?'

'She's fine, fine.' Muller sighed. 'The man who tried to kill you is dead. Do you remember that?'

'Yes. Chet Harper.'

'Right. That's what they said his name was. Also, Chance Elson is dead.'

Marric met the doctor's gaze. 'Chance Elson?' he asked.

'Yes. Your sister killed him.' There was no disapproval in the man's tone. 'He tried to pull a pistol on her, so she shot him. The sheriff himself came out from Eugene to supervise the case. He didn't want any complications with Howard Elson over his son's death. The Elsons are pretty powerful in these parts, as I'm sure you know.'

'I know.'

'The sheriff cleared you and your sister. No charges are going to be pressed, it seems.'

'Where is she?'

'She's back in Jasper. She's supposed to be coming out to see you this afternoon.' The doctor studied Marric's face and realized the man wanted to be alone. 'I'll let you rest some more,' he said. 'I'll have the daughter bring you some soup a little later if you'd like.'

'That sounds real good, Doc. Thanks for everything.'

Muller waved and went out of the room, closing the door softly. Marric heard him and his daughter talking for a moment, then they moved away from the door. Marric put his head back against the pillows. Soon he fell asleep again.

* * *

Marijo came and saw him, and over the next few days he regained his strength. He got back on his feet and even rode his horse for a while. Then one morning he announced that he was ready to leave and return to Jasper. Doctor Muller tried to discourage him, but Marric was determined. He was, after all, still the marshal there, and there were prisoners in custody at his jail.

Marric and his sister stopped by the family property on their way into town. They stopped before their father's grave, neither speaking for a few minutes. Marric put his arm around Marijo.

'We're going to rebuild that house,' he said. 'I promise. We'll do it for Ma and Pa.'

She raised her face. 'They would like that.'

'This is still Marric land, and it's going to stay that way. They made a good life here, for themselves and for us. I owe it to them.'

They rode into Jasper and Marric made straight for the law office. Gordon Jeffers was behind the desk, looking at a sheet of paper. He glanced up at Marric and rose to his feet, a smile spreading across his face.

'Damn good to see you, Jack!' he said.

'Thanks, Gordon. How've our guests been treating you?'

Jeffers looked toward the cell block door and smiled.

'They been real quiet, particularly since they heard about what happened to Chance Elson and his cousin.'

'I ain't surprised. I think they were doing Chance's bidding when they went for Burt. Maybe it'll all come out at the trial.'

'Yeah, it might.'

'Either way, they've got a date with the hangman.'

Jeffers walked over to the desk and picked up the piece of paper he had been reading.

'I think you'll find this interesting, Jack,' he said, handing it to Marric.

It was a Wanted dodger, sent out a week before, offering a $500 reward for Chet Harper. Marric read it carefully, then handed it back to Jeffers.

'Murdered two girls in Klamath Falls,' he said. He thought of the horrors that his parents had experienced in their final moments, and of what Marijo might have experienced.

'I'll be damned.'

Jeffers sighed. 'You know they had Burt's funeral day before yesterday?'

'Yeah. Marijo told me.'

'Mayor had his room cleaned up. It'll be ready for the next marshal.'

Marric adjusted his gun belt. 'Well, Gordon, I'm ready to take over again. You done me a mighty big favor.'

'It was nothing,' Jeffers said casually, shrugging into his coat. He donned his Stetson and shook Marric's hand. 'I'll be seeing you, Marshal.'

He left, and Marric watched him make his way down the street. He picked up the keys off the desk and checked on the men in the cell block. Golding was the only one awake; he watched Marric warily. His old cocksureness was nowhere in evidence. Marric wondered if the little cowpunch had begun to grasp the gravity of his situation.

The marshal returned to the office. The day passed quietly, as usual. After his evening rounds, Marric stopped in at the hotel. Marijo would be staying there indefinitely until she found more permanent lodgings. He saw that she was comfortably settled in, and then, after a brief visit, he returned to the law office for the night.

He had set up the cot by the desk and was preparing to turn in when he heard someone tap on the door. When he opened it, he was startled to see Howard Elson standing before him.

'Can I come in, Marshal?' Elson asked.

'Yes, sir,' Marric said solemnly. He moved aside and the old rancher stepped inside. Marric closed the door and turned to Elson. 'What can I do for you?'

'I've heard about everything that happened,' Elson said slowly, looking down at his hands. 'I was friends with your ma and pa since before you was born. I'm sorry about everything that happened.' He raised his eyes. 'I don't hold anything against you or your sister for what happened to Chance. If he was involved like the sheriff said, then he got what he deserved.'

He put his hand out; Marric didn't hesitate to shake it.

'Thank you, Howard,' he said.

Nearly overcome by emotion, Elson nodded and left without saying anything more.

Marric slept badly, turning things over in his mind. In the morning, he walked down to the cafe and got a pot of coffee. The mayor was waiting for him out front of the office when he returned.

As they greeted each other, Marric noted the look of concern in the man's face.

Smith said, 'Jack, I — I, uh, don't know what to say.'

Marric patted his shoulder. 'There's not really much to say, Mayor. What's done is done. The only thing that matters to me now is that Marijo is alive, and safe.'

'Yes, yes,' Smith agreed. 'Thank God!'

'There was something I wanted to talk to you about,' Marric added.

'Go ahead.'

'I heard the sheriff is going to send a deputy out to take over here until a permanent marshal is found.'

Smith nodded. 'Yes, that's been arranged now. It took some doing.'

'Well, if it's all the same to you, Mayor, I'd like to keep the job. On a permanent basis.'

The surprised mayor smiled. 'I think I speak for all the residents of Jasper when I say that would be most welcome. Yes, sir — most welcome.'

'Thank you, Mayor. We can work out all the details soon.'

'Will you be wanting Burt's quarters?'

Marric looked toward the stairs that led up to the small apartment.

'Yes,' he said. 'They're for the marshal, ain't they? I just hope I can fill Burt's boots.'

★ ★ ★

The following weeks passed quickly.

Bill Golding, Hal Clement, and Jack Campbell were tried in Eugene for the murder of Burt Kroll. All three denied involvement, but they were found guilty and sentenced to death. They were hanged the next day.

Marijo Marric returned to work at the school-house in Jasper.

Jack Marric stayed on as marshal. A year after taking the job, he finished rebuilding his parents' house.

We do hope that you have enjoyed reading this large print book.

Did you know that all of our titles are available for purchase?

We publish a wide range of high quality large print books including:
Romances, Mysteries, Classics
General Fiction
Non Fiction and Westerns

Special interest titles available in large print are:
The Little Oxford Dictionary
Music Book, Song Book
Hymn Book, Service Book

Also available from us courtesy of Oxford University Press:
Young Readers' Dictionary
(large print edition)
Young Readers' Thesaurus
(large print edition)

For further information or a free brochure, please contact us at:
Ulverscroft Large Print Books Ltd.,
The Green, Bradgate Road, Anstey,
Leicester, LE7 7FU, England.
Tel: (00 44) **0116 236 4325**
Fax: (00 44) **0116 234 0205**